ALL WE KNOW

By the same author

Hey Phantom Singlet
Cannily Cannily

ALL WE KNOW

Simon French

ANGUS
& ROBERTSON
PUBLISHERS

*Publication assisted by the
Literature Board of the Australia Council,
the Federal Government's arts funding
and advisory body.*

ANGUS & ROBERTSON PUBLISHERS

*Unit 4, Eden Park, 31 Waterloo Road,
North Ryde, NSW, Australia 2113, and
16 Golden Square, London W1R 4BN,
United Kingdom*

*First published in Australia
by Angus & Robertson Publishers in 1986
First published in the United Kingdom
by Angus & Robertson (UK) Ltd in 1987*

Copyright © Simon French 1986

*National Library of Australia
Cataloguing-in-publication data.*

*French, Simon, 1957-
  All we know.*

  ISBN 0 207 15359 0.

  I. Title.

A823'.3

Printed in Singapore

This book was written with the assistance of the Literature Board of the Australia Council.

For some people I used to know well.

ONE

Morning assemblies at school are really boring.

I'm glad I hid in the classroom during sport on Friday. And Mr Clifton knew, but he never said anything.

There's a message about me on the classroom wall, and I bet Sean Taylor wrote it.

At last, Arkie found a point at which she could wedge herself into the conversations around her.

"What's high school like?" she asked in a hopeful voice.

The adults seated around the dinner table fell silent for exactly five seconds, and then all seemed to chorus, "Awful! Terrible!" and either fell about laughing or returned to the conversations they'd been having before she'd interrupted.

Great. Thanks.

The young man across the table said to her, "Best time of your life. Wonderful kids —" He swept an arm expansively about the table, "— talented teachers. What more can I say?"

Arkie couldn't remember his name, even though he'd been around for dinner before. *Alex? Alan?*

Mum leaned her chin on one hand and said, "Alan, you're not giving my daughter the wrong idea about that marvellous place we work in, are you?" Some wine from her glass dribbled onto the tablecloth. Earlier in the evening, one of the other adults had tried coaxing mum into playing some songs on the piano, but she'd refused. "Second period tomorrow, I've got Year Seven," mum had replied caustically. "Come up and hear me trying to instil in them some sense of melody and rhythm."

So music had rattled and thudded on the stereo instead.

Alan the teacher pressed a hand to his chest. "Would I give anyone the wrong idea about school?" he said to Arkie's mum in an earnest voice, "Of course not. She might wind up in my English class next year or something."

"Aaargh," gurgled mum, and the two of them launched into some school-related horror story.

Even with just mum and Michael here, it's like school twenty-four hours a day. Mum and Michael would bandy names between them, discussions about high school pupils unknown to Arkie. Or mum would gripe about staff meetings with Michael sitting at the kitchen table marking overdue history essays; the pair of them preparing work stencils and drinking lots of coffee.

And right now, there were twelve or more teachers sitting around a table of food-emptied plates, because it was Michael's birthday. He was at the head of the table talking about something complicated with Glenda, who was a school counsellor.

Teachers. I'm surrounded by teachers. Arkie leaned back on her chair and gazed about. *But it's good having visitors.* She liked the extra company, the noise and hum of voices and laughter. Someone, once, had built the house for people and parties; had left this downstairs room open and expansive, the upstairs bedrooms cubbyholed and the walls lined with windows. Because it was night time, the view outside was of streetlights, curtained lights from the home units down the road and the distant glare of floodlights over the walkway next to the beach.

Here inside, there was the sharp, sweet smell of wine and a haze of cigarette smoke above the table. Opposite, in his own chair, Jo's eyes were dropping closed and his head started to droop. Someone pointed him out to mum, who answered, "Hmm, I know. It's way past his bedtime."

Then someone else put a Midnight Oil tape into the stereo and turned it up too loudly, so that Jo jerked awake once more and stared dreamily about.

"Thirty-two today!" one of the women at the other end of the table chanted. Michael opened his mouth in a silent scream and pretended to tear his hair out.

Mum sighed to herself, then stood up and walked around to where Jo was sitting. He was falling asleep again and she picked him up, hitching him onto one hip. "Jo's bedtime, everyone," she announced, waving his hand for him and adding in a squeaky Jo voice, "Goodnight everybody."

They chorused noisily back, as Michael stood

up to plant a farewell kiss on Jo's forehead. Then Jo buried his face in mum's shoulder and she heaved him upstairs.

Big baby.

The table conversations resumed their course. The stories were interesting and funny to listen to, but Arkie wished patiently that someone would involve her in the talking as well. First thing that evening she'd had the routine questions, as everyone arrived with their packets of savoury biscuits and wine casks. *How old are you now? What's school like? What do you like doing in your spare time, then?* And it seemed that her answers had all fitted into a five-minute bracket and that they'd been the sort of answers people were expecting anyway.

Resigned, she looked away. Her gaze rested on the piano in the far corner of the loungeroom. The lid was down and there was sheet music lying on top in uneven piles, along with an old reel-to-reel tape recorder. The floor around bustled with electric leads, two microphones on stands and a small, ancient school desk whose top was occupied by a keyboard synthesizer. It was here that mum doodled, experimented and composed. It was this part of the house that provided background soundtracks to all other activities. Mum and her music had been entwined ever since Arkie could remember.

"Nearly bedtime for you as well," came her mum's voice beside her.

Arkie pretended not to hear.

"Bedtime soon," mum repeated quietly.

"Not too soon," Arkie murmured, determined to stay awake and about at least until the birthday cake and cups of coffee were brought out.

TWO

Some kind of noise had woken her.

Dazed and heavy-eyed, Arkie blinked and stared into the room's darkness, until her sight adjusted and began to pick out the shapes of things. The night sky shimmered through the windows next to the wardrobe, and wiry treetops and clouds were illuminated by the struggling moon. On the wall opposite, she could just make out Jo's school paintings and beneath them, the shape of his bed.

On impulse, she kicked her quilt back and stepped onto the floor. The room's layout she knew by heart and in the darkness, could pick her way around the edge of the matting, the corner of her bed, the chairs and work table with unfinished homework still there, and the floorboard with the jagged edge of splinters. *There's Lego on the floor here somewhere, I know it.* She trod warily across to the windows, her feet half anticipating the jab of a plastic block. But there proved nothing unexpected to tread on, and she could hear no more conversation from downstairs, either. Everyone must have left.

6

Something had woken her. At first she had thought it might have been Goodvibes the cat, making his lazy way around the room in search of somewhere to sleep. Or maybe it was Jo in his bed, erupting into a snuffling snore as he often tended to do. Beyond the doorway was a faint hint of light from the loungeroom downstairs and suddenly, an even fainter hint of music — swirling, ebbing electric music that whispered through the house, like the wind when it blew up from the sea and hissed around the walls and windows.

She always plays this quiet stuff at night.

The music stopped for a moment, and Arkie heard the click of the reel-to-reel being switched on. The synthesiser whispered into life again. Her mum was committing a new melody to tape.

Outside, the orange haze of sodium streetlights hung lazily in the darkness above the main road. Outlines of buildings were highlighted and beyond the row of pine trees along the beach's edge, the ocean began and ended indeterminately. If she had pushed the window wide, Arkie would probably have been able to hear the rise and fall of waves in the distance, but the night's chill was seeping through onto her arms and chest and she made her way back to bed.

Downstairs, the hushed music continued. Arkie slithered back under the quilt, and almost immediately there was an abrupt impact, as Goodvibes leapt up onto the bed. His paws probed around for a suitable resting place, padded across Arkie's stomach and onto the space next to her feet. He flopped himself down and started purring.

7

"Stupid cat," Arkie mumbled, and fell asleep to the sound of her mother's music.

The half-light sent her eyes blinking open as a ray of sun found her face and brightened the shadows around. Too sleepy to move so that she could read the time on the bedside clock, Arkie gazed at the limited view that she lay facing; Jo still asleep underneath an Everest of bedclothes, and the Atrocity Cabinet over at one of the windows. Its mirrored shelves, once intended for crystal and glass, now held Arkie's bizarre collection of objects — the bird's nest she'd found on the vacant block next door, the dog's skull and frog skeleton found last year on holidays, her old Barbie doll with the missing leg, a snakeskin Michael had given her, and the collection of plastic souvenir snowstorms that she seemed to wind up with any time an aunt or her grandmother went away on holidays somewhere. Swaying surfers, ferry boats and skiing resorts were all imprisoned in their plastic bubbles.

They're really off, those things. That's why I like them.

"Horrible piece of furniture," mum had said when they'd first moved in with Michael, and the cabinet had been in the loungeroom, full of glasses and crockery. Arkie had to convince her not to relegate it to the cold, cobwebbed space under the house.

"Atrocity Cabinet," Michael had called it, once Arkie filled the mirrored shelves with her treasures. The name had stuck.

The bathroom door clicked shut and there was the squeak of taps and the rattle of the shower being turned on. Jo was out of bed and padding out of the room trailing school shorts and shirt, leaving behind a damp pile of pyjamas on the floor and the familiar smell of a wet bed. Arkie frowned and wrinkled her nose.

"Mess everywhere," she muttered, her voice half muted by sheets and quilt. "Lego and cars and clothes all over the place." In a louder voice, she added, "Come and clean your things up, you little grot."

There was no answer from her brother. The heavy lump that had been resting itself against her feet and legs all night stirred and shifted, as Goodvibes the cat stretched himself and sat up, realising that Jo had gone downstairs and that now was a good time to con some breakfast out of somebody. He gave his white and tabby fur a few cursory licks before springing off the bed and galloping out into the hallway and down to the kitchen.

In the near distance was the inevitable Monday morning hum of peak-hour traffic down on the main road. Then, abruptly, another noise commenced outside the window — an engine rumbling and chugging and the sound, she thought, of dirt being dug and dropped.

Roadworks? At this time of day? In a dead-end street?

When finally she got out of bed to look through the windows, she was startled to see the tussocked grass and native shrubs of the vacant block next door being levelled by a person on a bulldozer. "They're building something," she said to herself in a disappointed voice, because this was the last remaining vacant block on the whole of Ramsay Street.

The cul-de-sac spilled down the hill in a ragged run of grey bitumen. On either side were ranked blocks of flats, some very new, others showing the ready decay that a hastily built edifice seems to acquire quickly if it has pandered to a confusion of clever trends. Blond bricks had become stained with brown watermarks, and the fake wrought iron lacework on one building had lost most of its paint. The windows to the home units were often mere holes in blank walls, their only individuality being the colour of the curtains behind them. The footpaths in front of the units were invariably decorated with a line of plastic garbage bins, and the grass between the path and the street was invariably neatly mown and trimmed.

But here, at the end of the cul-de-sac, the buffalo grass had straggled over into the guttering and spread uninhibited into the foliage and undergrowth of the vacant block. It was where a lot of local kids rode their bikes or played chasing and hiding games, this welcome and unruly break between Arkie's house and the shock of concrete, bricks and steel that was the remainder of the street.

Not any more. What's happening to it now?

The alarm clock in mum's and Michael's room rang out shrilly. There was a bang and clatter as someone's hand sent it tumbling to the floor, and

10

then more thumps as the same hand sought to kill the bell.

I bet that's Michael. He always sleeps in.

Finally the sound expired. Arkie heard the creak of the bathroom door, the slap of footsteps into the next-door bedroom and then her mum giggling.

"Stop laughing, I'm dying," came Michael's voice, and then he walked past Arkie's doorway and down to the kitchen.

"Urk. Monday," Arkie told herself and eventually wandered downstairs in her school uniform.

In the kitchen, Michael was at the fridge carrying out hangover-reduction measures with a great many glasses of orange juice. On the sink, another glass contained water and a fizzing red tablet.

In the loungeroom, the devastation was complete. Glasses half-full, empty and overturned, ashtrays full of dingy butts, the remains of chips and dips, the stereo power light still glowing on, the tape deck having patiently progressed to the end of a cassette.

"Some party," Arkie marvelled aloud.

"Sunday night parties are bloody deadly things," Michael said from behind the fridge door. "In fact, they probably should be illegal."

"It was your birthday," Arkie replied.

The air had a bittersweet aftertaste of tobacco and wine about it. Jo wandered in from outside, where he'd been watching the progress of the bulldozer on the vacant block. "They're gonna build something," he stated emphatically. "We

11

won't be able to ride our bikes there any more."
His hair was spiky and straggly, a bit like the
paintbrushes Arkie used in art at school, and his
face still had a crease mark from where he'd had
his head buried in his pillow all night. He paused
to look at Arkie, Michael and then the room. "It's a
bit messy in here," he added.

Michael clasped a hand to his forehead and
said, "Jo, how would you like to earn some extra
pocket money?"

"Yeah, sure."

"Well then, you can pretend to be the human
vacuum cleaner and —"

"I know, I know — clean up."

"You guessed it. Glasses in the sink, ashtrays
emptied, tapes back in their boxes, etcetera,
etcetera. You're an old hand at this sort of thing.
You can help too, Arkie."

"Not me. I like watching other people work."

"How much you gonna pay me?" Jo asked
Michael.

"Depends on the job. For an utterly supreme
effort, I'd say a dollar."

"That's okay, I guess," Jo said, narrowing his
eyes and slowly considering. He started collecting
glasses and ferrying them to the sink. "Mum said
to remind you it's your turn this week to give me
and Arkie our lunch money."

"Oh," Michael said, easing himself into an
armchair near the stereo and sipping from the
glass containing the dissolved red tablet, "yeah."

"The canteen had a price rise last week and
everything costs more now," Jo added in a hopeful

tone. "Isn't that right, Arkie?"

Arkie was getting out bowls and cutlery for breakfast. "Yeah," she answered in a non-committal voice. Goodvibes was at her feet yowling and complaining. Out of the kitchen window, she could see Headley, the labrador bull terrier cross, staring back at her. He was on the back porch and doing his best to look starved and neglected.

"Did you have a good birthday?" Jo asked. He was kneeling on the floor by now, matching up cassettes with their cases.

"Oh, it was a ripper," Michael answered in a deadpan voice. "It's just that I have to go to work today. I have to discuss George Orwell novels with dopey year nine kids . . ."

"Huh. I had my birthday on a school day last year."

"Poor lad."

"You had a good party, but. Heaps of people."

"Yeah. Hope we didn't keep you kids awake."

"I stayed awake listening to that man Alan telling rude jokes —"

"Aw, you did not, Jo," Arkie interrupted, "you were fast asleep."

"Was not."

"You were dead as a doornail. I heard mum playing music, really late. I think she was taping something."

"I was awake," Jo protested. Michael was slumped in his chair, eyes closed and gripping his forehead, and Jo suddenly seemed to think better of pursuing the conversation. He resumed sorting

13

out the cassettes. Arkie drowned a couple of Weetbix with milk and carried the bowl across to the windows, where she resumed watching the bulldozer's steady, noisy work.

Mum came downstairs, dressed and ready for the day ahead. "Right, Jo, how about some breakfast? Leave the cleaning up for after. Arkie, this isn't a takeaway bar; can you sit down while you're eating?"

"I'm watching the bulldozer."

"No time for that now. We have to leave in an hour. And when you've finished breakfast, go and change those earrings, please."

"Aw why?"

Her protest seemed to go unheard, because in the space of ten seconds, mum had switched the kettle on and made a lightning trip into the laundry to retrieve a favourite pair of sneakers. She laced them up kneeling on the floor near the fridge, so that Goodvibes thought he was about to be given breakfast. "Has anyone fed this blasted cat yet?" mum asked, fending Goodvibes away with one hand. "Probably not," she added to herself.

At last, she stood up and took a more leisurely walk over to one of the loungeroom mirrors. "Huh," she said, taking a mouthful of orange juice from the glass Michael had left on a cupboard top, "at least I don't need eye makeup today. My eyes are shadowy already."

"And bloodshot," Arkie called from over at the kitchen table. "I reckon you've both got really big hangovers, except mum's better at pretending she hasn't." She made the last remark to Jo who was now sitting next to her, and he bent his head over his bowl, shuddering and trying hard not to spit his cereal out through his giggles.

"You finish your breakfast," mum said, smirking. "I'm not admitting to anything, Arkie Gerhardt."

Michael was still sprawled in the armchair. "Where do you get your energy from?" he asked mum.

"My natural enthusiasm for work," she answered, leaning from behind the armchair and looping her arms around his shoulders. "You look awful."

"I feel awful. I feel like wagging school."

"You lazy thing. What classes have you got today?"

"A double with year seven, they're okay. Um . . . one with year eleven, passable. A double with year nine, they're hopeless. Couldn't debate their way out of a paper bag. Totally uninspiring. I might stay home."

"If I can make it to school, so can you!" mum responded, digging him gently in the ribs.

"I'm a sick man!"

Arkie finished breakfast.

"Earrings!" mum reminded her loudly, because the noise from the bulldozer next door seemed to be increasing.

"Why can't I wear these ones?"

"Because they're not safe things to wear to school. I don't want you coming home from school with an ear lobe missing because some stupid kid's decided to grab you by a dangling earring. That's why."

15

"Kylie wears them."

"I don't —" mum started to say, but stopped short. "Just go and change them, please."

Quite abruptly, the bulldozer was switched off.

"Peace at last," Michael said.

Arkie clattered upstairs, and on the way called back, "Well there's a really big mess in our room and I reckon Jo should get up here and do some cleaning up." No-one answered.

She muttered to herself, took the feather earrings out, tucked them into the pocket of her school dress and went to rifle through some drawers in her wardrobe. *I left some pocket money somewhere.*

The first few drawers yielded neither spare change or replacement earrings. And when she reached the middle drawer she paused, because here was where she kept things her father sent her.

It was also where the smelly soaps and talcum powders were kept, things her grandmother insisted on giving her for birthdays and Christmas and that Arkie never got around to using. There was a collection of every merit card she'd ever gained at school, almost from kindergarten on. These had the school crest printed in brown, the headmistress's signature and typewritten comments like *Improving her handwriting, A good class helper* and *Arkie used her best manners today.* Long ago, when she brought that last one home, mum had raised an eyebrow, narrowed one eye and said at length, "Hmm."

There were other things in this drawer too, all sorts of odds and ends — bubblegum cards, an autograph book, and badges of all sorts. The post and birthday cards from her father she glanced through occasionally, but always by herself, quietly and thoughtfully. Sometimes the cards had been late, and one year he'd missed altogether. The cards usually contained money. This year Arkie had written back, "Dear dad, thank you for the card you sent. I used the money for tights and a dress. By the way, it was my twelfth birthday, not my eleventh. Love from Arkie."

I only wrote that letter in February. Only four months ago. It seems like ages.

There was also a cassette tape her father had once sent; a recorded letter and birthday message in his pausing, gravelly voice. In a conversation that sounded more like dialogue between business colleagues, he spoke about life and work in distant Perth and said that he hoped Arkie would keep working hard at school and be a help at home.

Huh.

The cards were better, with no listening involved. At age six, she had still remembered the sound of his voice clearly. Now, when she played the cassette through or spoke to him during his rare phone calls and even rarer visits to Sydney, it was strange equating his voice with the face in some photos — the wedding ones mum didn't keep with the newer snapshots.

"Aha," she mumbled, finding a pair of stud earrings.

Jo received birthday cards too, and the

attraction for him was probably only the folded money within. The cards he'd sit up on his chest of drawers, along with his toy cars and Lego constructions, until they blew onto the floor or slid down against the wall. *Jo was still a baby when we moved in here, so he hardly knows dad at all.*

"I see my dad a bit," Kylie had answered when Arkie had quizzed her at school one day. "He has access once a month, and we go out somewhere."

"How is it? Seeing him, I mean."

"It's okay," Kylie had answered in her usual non-committal manner. "At least him and mum don't argue every time they see each other now."

Arkie creaked the drawer shut once more. Her comprehensive search for money had been less than successful.

Later, when Michael had donned a jacket and stuffed his briefcase full of students' books, he was still mumbling, "I'd really like to stay at home today."

"I'm making it to school after a late night," Jo announced righteously.

"Have you finished breakfast yet?" mum enquired, waiting for toast to spring from the temperamental toaster.

"Nearly. Even though Miss Sereni shouts a lot, I'm going to school."

"Only because your class are horrors," Arkie said.

Outside, the bulldozer rumbled into life again. Mum grimaced. Michael frowned. "I don't like the look of what's happening next door," he said glumly.

"Block of flats?" mum said. It was a statement rather than a question, really.

Michael nodded. "More than likely. Our luck's run out. Bang goes the view."

"Can't we do anything about it?" Arkie asked.

"Not much," mum said. "If we owned this house, we could lodge an objection of some sort with the local council. Because we're renting, there's not a lot we can do. And if whatever's getting built next door is too many storeys high, there won't be much for us to look at, either. Brick walls and other people's windows."

"Yuk," Arkie replied.

"Whose turn to wash up this morning?" mum asked, passing the slowly recovering Michael a plate of toast.

Arkie pointed at herself. "I don't have t' do all the party stuff as well, do I?"

"Just the glasses. We'll tackle the rest after school. Jo, when you've finished, I wanted wet sheets and pyjamas put into the washing machine, please."

"Good," Arkie said quietly as she filled the sink with soapy water. There had been lots of times recently when she'd felt the bedroom shared with Jo crowded her out. Irritated, she began dunking glasses into the water and leaving them to drain beside her.

Behind came Michael's quiet voice, "Another wet night, mate?"

"Yeah," Jo answered soberly, standing up to deposit his breakfast things on the sink, "I didn't wake up in time."

"Ah well...better luck tonight." There was a

chart on the back of the pantry door that Michael
had drawn up with textas, to look like a calendar.
The heading on it said "Dry Nights", and gold
stars were supposed to go up every time the goal
was realised. There weren't very many gold stars
so far.

Once, when Jo had made the same glum reply
to Michael's asking, Arkie had retorted flippantly,
"God, Jo, one day you'll float down the stairs and
out the front door!" Michael's response to this still
made her wince when she recalled it; the way he'd
sighed and reprimanded her quietly but firmly.
"Arkie, that was a bit cruel," he'd said. "I used to
wet the bed too, when I was Jo's age, and it wasn't
much fun. You couldn't go staying with friends.
Missed out on school camps, scared the other kids
would find out. My dad used to belt me for it. I'm
trying to help Jo — how about you helping too?"

I can't stand the smell of wet beds. But she
remained determined not to comment aloud about
it again.

My dad used to belt me for it. It was something
Arkie had heard from kids at school or read about
in books. *Our family isn't like that. Mum and
Michael nag, but they don't belt.*

She turned around. Michael was sipping
coffee and Jo had nuzzled up close to him, the way
he often did. "Hey Michael," Jo was saying softly,
"you forgot to shave this morning."

"I'm going for the rugged look," Michael
replied, jiggling his eyebrows up and down. A peal
of laughter came from the spare room next to the
stairs where mum was hunting up a textbook for
school.

"It's the truth," Michael protested. Mum laughed again.

"Your face feels like sandpaper," Jo informed him.

"And your face looks like it's been attacked by vegemite on toast," Michael replied, pushing Jo away gently. "Go upstairs and clean up."

My dad used to belt me for it. When she replayed that statement to herself, a lot of questions she'd never before asked came to mind. *I've never met Michael's parents. I don't even know where he grew up.*

The air outside was heavy with the smell of diesel fumes, and the bulldozer by now was labouring at the bottom corner of the vacant block.

"Save me from Mondays and year nine," Michael croaked as he shut the front door.

"Sorry!" mum said, striding briskly ahead towards the carport. "There's no escape! Listen to my Monday, Mike: I've got a parent to see and three lots of stencils to run through that crummy duplicator before school. I've got three double periods today, one of them with Masher McMullan and his mates in year eight. I've —"

"I get the point," Michael interrupted.

Arkie and Jo had sidetracked down into the backyard for a closer look at the bulldozer's activities. The grassy, bushy landscape was being transformed into a large rectangle of dry, bare earth.

"Oi!" mum called from the carport, "I'm leaving, now. If you want a lift to school, hurry up."

Pockets jingling with lunch money, Arkie and Jo sprinted up to the car. First in the carport was Michael's old utility, which at one time must have been quite flash, but had been reduced by age and salt air to a rust-spotted, cobwebbed heap. Michael hardly drove it any more, but insisted on keeping it.

Behind the utility was mum's car, the black Citroen.

A shark on wheels. Mum was endeared to it, called it the Batmobile, and even got around to washing it every so often. The black paint had been affected in places by corroding salt air, the dashboard vinyl was cracked with old age and the chrome of the rear bumper was obliterated by political and environmental stickers.

"Come on," mum said with real impatience. "In, in."

They clambered in, slammed the doors shut and then had to wait a moment longer as Michael raced back inside for his briefcase.

"How could you possibly forget that?" mum asked wearily when he returned.

"Quite easy when you're as unwell as me," he managed to smirk in reply. Mum spun the motor into life and reversed the car onto the street.

Wow, I hate Monday mornings. They're always like this — rush, rush, rush.

They cruised down the steep part of the hill, past the ranks of home units and numerous other kids from school who were by now appearing in doorways and ambling down footpaths. At the intersection to the main road, they paused for a break in the traffic.

Cars, buses and motorbikes hissed and rumbled past in both directions. Arkie stared ahead, past mum, Michael and the car's windscreen to the beach and ocean that lay on the opposite side of the main road.

It was barely ten minutes' walk from home, and yet Arkie hardly ever ventured near the beach and the water. Swimming had never appealed to her much, and, anyway, some days the water was so crowded with driftwood and litter that it barely seemed like the blue ocean she saw on postcards.

THREE

The walled spaces between the shops were cluttered with peeling concert posters and spray-painted messages that said things like TRACEY & JEFF 4 EVER and AMERICAN BASES OUT. Yet another said DANIEL G. IS A, with a concluding word angrily obliterated by paint of another colour. Arkie, Jo and all the other kids passed this graffiti every day on their way home from school, and no longer read the messages out aloud to each other in laughing voices. They barely even noticed them. The shopping centre sat opposite the beach, flanked by No Parking signs and the trees the local council had only recently thought to plant. Every afternoon, the kids passed the supermarket, the milkbar, the bakery, the service station and video hire bar and the chemical warmth of the dry cleaners. The Parade Hotel sat monumental at the end of all this. At weekends, it reverberated to the rumble of live bands, but during the week, a muted soundtrack of clinking glasses and the rasp of a tired jukebox escaped through the swinging glass doors. Arkie's inquisitive gaze sometimes met the eyes of the sombre-faced regulars who sat inside at the hotel's footpath windows, temporarily distracted from racing form guides to the view through the glass at the world outside.

"Me and Rebecca came down here on Sunday night," Kylie Bethel said. "We stood out on the footpath and watched the band that was playing inside. Didn't we, Rebecca?"

"Yeah."

You've only told us about a hundred times, Kylie.

"And then these guys in a panel van drove up and started calling out to us, so we bolted back to Rebecca's flat." A smile lingered on Kylie's face, as if daring Arkie to talk about her own Sunday evening.

We were having Michael's birthday party.
"That sounds really exciting," Arkie said, deadpan.

"It was!" Rebecca answered with annoying enthusiasm, and she laughed with Kylie. Other conversations buzzed noisily amongst the group of kids as they strolled along the footpath, dragging and swinging schoolbags along, and milling at shop window displays.

Kylie pointed at one of the items in the window of the casual and surf clothing boutique. "My mum's buying me that," she said in the competitive voice she increasingly used.

Rebecca shooed her blond plaits behind her head and considered this remark in silence. Other kids walked on by, their reflections sweeping along the shopfront glass. "What doesn't your mum buy you?" Sean Taylor said derisively.

Arkie had stopped on the footpath next to Kylie and Rebecca, looking at their reflected faces and listening blankly to their conversation. Kylie's hair hung in blow-waved flounces around her face. "She looks like one of those *femmes fatale* you see on American soap operas," Michael had once remarked, and traitorously, gleefully, Arkie had laughed.

"Hey," Rebecca said, "what about those boots Mr Clifton wore to school today?"

"Those pointy ones?" Kylie answered, picking up her schoolbag and walking on.

"Yeah. He wears some great clothes sometimes."

"Great? Weird, I reckon."

Arkie rolled her eyes and commented, "At least he isn't boring, like some teachers at school."

"Yeah," said Rebecca, agreeing.

"I guess," Kylie said, shrugging.

Sean Taylor had doubled back along the footpath, running up to Arkie and saying noisily, "Hey, Ark, Adam wants you t' be his girlfriend!"

Sean's clothes always seemed to smell of lemon laundry detergent. Arkie wrinkled her nose and took a step away. "Get out of it!" she growled.

Sean ignored that. He yelled back at the kids down the road, "Hey, I told her!"

Adam Black, the smallest person in sixth class, was being nudged by Sean, Jo and a couple of the others. "Oooh aah, Adam, now we know . . ."

Adam jabbed a finger in the air and swung his schoolbag at some nearby feet. There were squeals and abuse as the group scattered themselves

26

across the footpath. An adult pedestrian tried to negotiate her way past, and shot the kids an annoyed look.

Sean said, "Hey, c'mon Ark, aren't you going to tell Adam how much you like him?"

Arkie made a face. "Urk, are you kidding?"

"How much you adore him?"

"Shut up, Taylor," Arkie said, aware that Jo was enjoying every minute of the reckless match-making that involved most of Arkie's class at school. "I'll tell your mummy that you got into trouble at school today, otherwise."

"Ark, Ark," Sean replied, making it sound like a bird squawk, "Ark, Ark —" He produced a thick texta from a pocket of his schoolbag, and strolled over to a nearby bus stop seat. On the wooden painted surface, he started to write, *Arkie G. loves-*, but Arkie dashed over and grabbed the texta from him. "Kylie!" she yelled, and tossed it into the air. Kylie caught the texta and passed it on amongst the group — to Rebecca, Adam, Warren, Voula and Jo — so that it remained split seconds away from Sean's grasp. His previously gleeful voice had changed to a whine of annoyance. "Aw, give it here," he said every few seconds.

"Here, Warren!"

"Kylie, Kylie —"

"Pst, Voula —"

"Here!" Ian Koh shouted hopefully, but most of the kids gave him swift, derisive looks and otherwise ignored him, as they usually did.

Sean's texta continued its way from hand to hand, and Sean was getting cranky. "Give it here!"

he protested, as the kids made their loud, meandering way past the advertisement-plastered takeaway and milkbar. Suddenly Sean came to a standstill, and said loudly, "Hey, Checcutti, ya big wagger!"

Robert Checcutti was leaning in the doorway of his parents' shop, having missed a day of school altogether. "Me?" he inquired innocently, shifting his not inconsiderable weight from one foot to the other. "I've been sick, haven't I?"

"Sick?!"

"Pull the other one, Rob."

"I have so been sick!" Robert said with emphasis. "Ask me mum if you don't believe me." He jabbed a thumb towards the back of the shop, where his mother hovered behind a distant counter. "And I've been working all day, haven't I? Not like *some* people I could name." His forehead was glazed with perspiration, a legacy from time spent cooking and frying up chips. "And there was another car accident this morning, right here at the traffic lights, and I phoned the tow truckers first. Another twenty dollars spotting fee my way."

"Aw big deal," Sean answered, his concentration wandering back to the fact that his texta was still being passed around.

Arkie regained possession of it. "Here's a present for you, Robert," she said, and threw the texta to him. He promptly handed it back to Sean.

"Thanks, mate," Sean said with a grin.

"Thanks a lot," Arkie groaned, rolling her eyes. Sean was edging back towards his unfinished graffiti on the bus stop seat. "If you write a single thing about me, Taylor, you'll be really sorry," she told him.

"I'm really scared of you too, Arkie. Ark Ark." To Robert, Sean said in a pointed voice, "See you at school tomorrow, Rob."

Robert's mother was silently beckoning him to return behind the counter. "See youse tomorrow," he called after them as they drifted on down the footpath again.

Arkie had started to walk with them, but realised then that Jo was no longer with her. He and Ian Koh had remained at the milkbar, and Jo was digging around in the pocket of his shorts.

"What's the hold-up?" she called.

"I'm playing the space invaders machine!" Jo shouted back. "Me and Ian are having a game."

"Yeah, and who's paying for it?" Arkie demanded.

"Me!" Jo replied, and anticipating criticism from his sister, added, "It's my money, and I can do whatever I like with it."

"Well, hurry up, then." Arkie frowned and sighed impatiently. The other kids had almost reached the corner of Ramsay Street. "See you later," she yelled.

Sean Taylor had temporarily abandoned completing his graffiti, but he compensated by yelling back, "Hey Arkie, Adam says he'll meet you behind the school library tomorrow!"

Adam Black shouted something rude, and clouted Sean in the back with his schoolbag. The last thing Arkie saw as they turned the corner was Kylie laughing about something to Rebecca.

I bet Kylie's going to Rebecca's place to play records or watch videos, Arkie leant against the wall between the milkbar and the supermarket with her schoolbag dumped on the ground beside her. The buses trundling past on the main road were full of schoolchildren and she fixed her gaze disinterestedly on the traffic and the passing faces contained within each vehicle. The sound of the sea hissed and filtered over the road. Tracksuit-uniformed joggers loped their way along the path that led between the arched, concreted surf life-saving club and the beach. In the nearby carpark, lurid panel vans and city-scarred station wagons sat, their occupants away in the water and hoping the surf would rise. Two men with windblown hair and in wetsuits swept past her into the Checcuttis' milkbar, their conversation a barrage of laughs and curses.

Arkie could see Jo and Ian sitting at the machine just inside the milkbar entrance. "Hurry up, Jo!" she called.

Ian Koh's face met hers at that remark, his dark, nervous eyes half-veiled by tassels of brown hair. He looked down again, at Jo who was sitting opposite and punching the machine's buttons.

"He's a strange boy," mum would say of Ian, usually after she'd wound up feeding him a meal, because his visits to the house were frequent and at odd hours.

"Undernourished," Michael once said softly and mysteriously. "His eyes look too big for his face. They always have."

30

It was the age difference that intrigued Arkie; Ian twelve and Jo four years younger: Ian quiet and morose, Jo devoted to his friend.

Spelling, maths, writing, natural science and more had left Arkie weary, and all she really wanted to do now was go home. "Hurry up," she grumbled as the boys straggled out of the milkbar minutes later. Jo pulled some faces behind her back.

At the Ramsay Street corner, there was a spray of fine glass on the bitumen and in the gutter; pieces of orange and red tail light lens and a small piece of car grille trim.

"Some accident," Ian remarked softly, as Arkie stopped and dug around in the pocket of her school tunic. Finding what she was looking for, she replaced the feather earrings she'd worn at school with the ordinary studs mum had told her to wear.

"You always do that," Ian said.

"I'm gonna tell mum on you," Jo said. "That's three days this week you've worn those feather ones to school and mum told you not to. She always —"

"Jo, will you shut up?" Arkie answered crankily. "There's plenty of things I could dob on you about."

"Like what?"

"Like whoever it was that wrote 'MANIAC' and 'GUTTER BASHER' in white chalk on the tyres of mum's car. She still thinks Michael did it."

"Well, he did!" Jo protested.

"He did not," Arkie replied.

"Did so. I saw him. And anyway, I can't even spell 'MANIAC' and 'GUTTER BASHER'."

Probably not. Anyway, it sounds like the kind of thing Michael would do.

The other kids had dispersed towards their separate addresses and were still yelling conversations to each other from entrance doorways of the closely-spaced blocks of home units. The Seaview building, where Ian lived, was built in white brick and had tiny verandahs crammed with garden furniture, pot plants and washing. He didn't leave Arkie and Jo at the Seaview's brick fence, and Arkie didn't really expect him to; he wandered home with them most afternoons once school was over.

At the far end of the street, where the steep hill concluded and the cliff and minor scrub began, the house was just visible. Its white weatherboard was caught in glimpses behind a tangle of trees and garden, and the rows of loungeroom and bedroom windows glared in the sun.

"I'm gonna go back down the road and play with Ian," Jo said suddenly. "We were gonna practise soccer kicks."

Arkie repressed the urge to say, "You and Ian can't play for peanuts," and answered instead, sharply, "You can't, Jo. Mum said you have to come straight home in the afternoon, and not to go anywhere until she and Michael get home."

"I want to —"

"MUM SAID," Arkie emphasised, and strode

on ahead so that Jo and Ian had to jog a few steps to catch up. The steep part of Ramsay Street was always a bit of an effort to climb, and the three of them trudged slowly up, past where the cement gutter had been damaged by the bulldozer, and past the levelled, vacant block where several workmen were measuring with tapes and string around excavated holes. There was one other house amongst Ramsay Street's ranks of home units, and that sat directly opposite the bulldozed block. It was a newish, mock-Spanish villa that was mostly concealed by a high white fence. Once or twice a day, the tall wooden gates were opened and a white Jaguar was driven out and down the street. From her upstairs bedroom, Arkie sometimes caught further glimpses of this neighbouring backyard and of the people who lived there; a husband, wife and young child who kept very much to themselves.

"You think you're the boss," Jo sneered at her as they walked through the carport and past Michael's utility. "Just because you're the oldest, you think you're smart." He darted away then, as if anticipating some sort of retaliation from Arkie. She gestured at him with a raised finger.

Goodvibes the cat was sitting on the doorstep and whining to be let in. He had bites taken out of his ears and scratches across his nose because the nights he didn't spend on Arkie's bed were spent in battle with other peoples' cats. "He leaves paw prints all over Michael's utility, and he pisses on the wheels of mum's car," Arkie heard Jo loudly inform visiting playmates from school one day.

33

"Get inside, stupid," she said to Goodvibes, opening the front door with her key. He scooted inside and waited beside the fridge in the kitchen.

"What's on TV?" Ian asked.

"Dunno," Jo replied, ditching his bag in the middle of the hallway and following Ian into the loungeroom. "Let's check it out."

"Don't turn it up too loudly," Arkie grumbled as Jo flicked the switch and the televised racket began. "Come here, you greedy pig," she said to Goodvibes, and poured some milk into a bowl for him. At the sound of her voice, Headley started yelping from out in the backyard, his chain lead rattling on the cement path. She took out a handful of dog biscuits, and knelt beside him as he snorted and gobbled them down. When he finished, he started pawing, nuzzling and licking. "Urk, death breath," Arkie said, wrinkling her nose. Headley stared longingly at her with his piggy bull terrier eyes, and flicked his large fruit bat ears up, down and backwards. Arkie relented, unclipped the lead and let him trot inside. "Go and attack Jo and Ian," she said, which he promptly did, before bounding upstairs to the luxury of an afternoon nap on one of the beds.

Arming herself with a Mars Bar and an orange juice from the fridge, Arkie went upstairs also. She set the refreshments on the work table next to the windows and stooped down to remove her school socks and sneakers. The sound of the TV echoed up the staircase.

She pushed a window open and settled herself at the table. A breeze was rustling through the

34

trees and bushes in the side garden, and immediately beyond the fence could be seen the trenches that crisscrossed the vacant block. Piping and bags of cement sat in the backs of a utility and a truck that were parked over the footpath.

"...after we'd come home from footy practice..."

"...what'd the wife say...?"

"...one minute we were..."

Fragments of the workmen's conversations, friendly banter and occasional swearing reached the bedroom windows and Arkie's hearing. They'd been working there for about a week now, and she was beginning to recognise their faces as they arrived each morning and left each afternoon.

"Four home units," one of them told Michael when he had leant over the fence one morning and asked what was being built, "only two storeys high. Shouldn't wreck your view over-much, mate."

"Huh," Michael had mumbled, not convinced entirely. After years of not having neighbours right next door, he knew it would be different enough when the units were built and people were living there.

They'll be able to spy on us. I'll be able to spy on them.

The bedroom windows offered a staggeringly good view of Ramsay Street. From her seat at the work table, Arkie could see directly into the loungeroom of Sean Taylor's flat, because his block of units was on the other side of the vacant block. She could see the large truck that belonged

35

to Adam Black's dad and was always parked in the very same spot. At weekends, she knew whenever Voula's Greek relatives were visiting, because the kerb would be jammed with shiny cars from another suburb, and there would be a dozen or so immaculately dressed children playing in the front yard of the units where Voula lived. Sometimes, she spotted Kylie's father arriving at weekends to take her out, and later dropping her off home again. There were groups of high school kids too, who sat on front fences on Saturdays and Sundays and paced up and down to the shopping centre and the beach. And right now, there were a couple of kids from Arkie's class at school lazily riding pushbikes in a meandering course down the centre of the road.

There was homework to do, courtesy of Mr Clifton, but Arkie postponed that. "Later," She said, and gazed wearily about the bedroom. A pillow and quilt were deposited on the floor, and Jo's bed was once more stripped of wet sheets. Matchbox cars and stencils from school littered a portion of the floor, and a good deal of the work table's space was occupied by Jo's textas and assorted activity books. "Mess everywhere. I'm really sick of it," she mumbled. Headley, thinking he was being spoken to, started whipping his tail on the bed and looked up expectantly. Arkie tossed him the remaining portion of her Mars Bar, which he wolfed down in about two seconds. "Lucky for you I'm generous," she said to him, and looked over at the blank wall beside her bed. Bits of Blu-Tack still clung to the places where she'd taken down the horse and rock-star pictures. They hadn't meant all that much to her, except that every other bedroom belonging to someone from school seemed to have been decorated the same way. Now she wasn't sure what to fill the plastered emptiness with. *Maybe some Japanese art prints, like the ones Mum and Michael have in the loungeroom. Except they cost money.*

Outside came the sound of the Batmobile humming into the driveway and under the carport, doors being opened and closed; mum's and Michael's voices.

"Can me and Ian go and play soccer?" Jo was inquiring loudly when Arkie reached the downstairs hallway.

Mum and Michael were depositing briefcases and schoolbooks on the hallway table. "Thank you for asking, dear," she said, pointedly answering a non-existent question, "I had a wonderful day. How about you?"

"Can we?" Jo asked again.

Mum walked into the kitchen. "No, because it's getting rather cold outside. Why don't you find something to do indoors? Apart from TV, that is. Go and turn the wretched thing off."

"Aw . . ." Jo muttered.

"Any mail, Arkie?" Michael asked, collapsing onto one of the kitchen chairs.

Headley had bounded into the kitchen. "And who let you in?" mum was saying.

"Two letters. One's a bill, I think."

"Oh goody. Wow, I'm dying for a cup of tea."

"You're dying for a cup of tea?" mum

37

responded, flicking the jug on. "I just feel like sleeping."

"Have a hard day or something?" Arkie asked.

Michael rolled his eyes around and tried to look demented. "Oh, you know, just the usual. Staff meetings. Ratty kids. Playground duty. How about you?"

"Well . . ." Arkie began, trying to forget about the walk home from school, "our class got into trouble at assembly today."

"Oh yeah?" Michael said, and he and mum chorused: "What for?"

"We all had to sing the school song, and Mr Clifton was pulling faces and making us giggle. Mrs King got really cranky with us."

"Hmm," said mum.

"School songs . . ." mumbled Michael.

"It was funny," Ian said, quietly smiling.

Jo was half-sitting on Michael's lap, and Ian had one arm timidly resting on Michael's shoulder. *Sometimes, Michael almost looks like he's Jo's dad.* Michael and Jo had the same tawny hair and they each had it cut in identical spiky, straggly lengths. *But Jo's eyes are like mine.* When Jo had first started school, older kids had come up to Arkie and sneered, "Hey, is your dad Japanese? You and your brother have got slanty eyes."

"Our dad's German," she had tried replying, but they had run away, disbelieving.

Our dad- Arkie looked at Ian. *No-one around here has ever seen your dad either, Ian. And everyone knows about your mother.* Ian's mother was someone Arkie occasionally sighted through

38

the hazy glass of the Parade Hotel, who dressed young but looked old, and left her home unit most days with people whose names Ian didn't know.

And she's down at the Parade right now. I know.

"It was funny on the way home today," Jo said, mainly to Michael. "Sean Taylor was writing things —"

"Shut up, Jo" Arkie interrupted quickly.

Mum shot her a frowning, curious look, and then said to Jo and Ian, "How about you guys going and finding something to do?"

"It was funny, but," Jo persisted.

"I don't think I want to hear it. Off you go."

Jo sidled out, with Ian in tow.

"What's up, Arkie?" Michael asked. "You look a bit glum."

"He's a pest."

"Who, Sean Taylor?"

"Him too. No, I mean Jo. I'm sick of looking after him all the time."

"Come on, Arkie," mum said patiently. "It's not all the time, it's after school for a short while, until Michael and I get home. That's all."

"Well it takes ages for us to get home in the afternoons sometimes, because he wants to stop and play space invaders or pinball machines or something," Arkie said in one breath. She could hear Jo and Ian clumping upstairs. "And he always leaves the bedroom in a mess. He's a pest, and I don't like looking after him like I have to."

"Arkie," mum continued, "Jo drives Michael and I around the bend sometimes as well. But he's

39

only eight and he is your brother. It's a responsibility you'll have to accept for a little while longer. There's no escaping responsibilities sometimes."

I'm not one of your high school pupils. Don't talk to me like that.

"Any homework tonight?" mum asked, trying to change the subject.

"Mmm. Social science and maths. It has to be done for tomorrow."

"Mr Clifton's starting to pile the work on, isn't he?" Michael said.

Arkie wrinkled her nose and said, "He reckons he's getting us ready for high school. It's really an excuse to make us work hard."

"Just out of interest," Michael continued, draining the last of his mug of tea, "when does Ian manage to do homework? He's either up here, or waiting outside the pub for his mum."

"He gets to school really early," Arkie replied, picking her schoolbag up from where she'd left it near the kitchen doorway, "and sits at his desk in the classroom and does it then. Sometimes he doesn't get it finished, but Mr Clifton lets him off."

Arkie went upstairs then, with the intention of getting some homework done, but Jo and Ian were each spread out on the bedroom floor, energetically sending matchbox cars skating across the matting into rattling collisions.

"Can't you go and play that somewhere else?" Arkie demanded sharply.

"This is my room, too," Jo replied just as sharply, "and anyway, mum says we're not allowed to play with cars downstairs."

"Well play something else, then!"

"We don't want to!"

"Ian, make him play somewhere else." But Ian wouldn't buy into the argument, and kept his gaze expectantly in Jo's direction. Arkie sighed in angry exasperation and returned downstairs.

"I can't work up there," she said, striding back into the kitchen, "Jo and Ian won't play anywhere else."

Mum and Michael were still seated at the kitchen table and leaning against each other in an affectionate, work-weary manner. Each of them sighed audibly, and mum said quietly, "You haven't had a very good day, have you?"

Arkie avoided a reply to that. "I just want to get my homework done."

"How about here or at the dining table?" mum suggested.

"I can't work with other people around. I have to be by myself or I can't concentrate."

Michael stood up. "Come and use the spare room," he said. "The desk in there's covered in junk —"

"The whole room's covered in junk," mum interrupted.

"— but I'll clear a space for you," he finished. "Come on."

The doorway near the base of the stairs opened into a room identical in confined size to the kitchen. The view through the only window was masked by overgrown shrubbery in the side garden. The floor was occupied by an ironing board, a pushbike belonging to Michael, and box upon box of textbooks and school equipment belonging to

41

both Michael and mum. Elsewhere on the floor were loose piles of books, the vacuum cleaner and a folded baby cot that Arkie and Jo each had used years before. Apart from pine bookshelves stacked with unruly piles of more books and other stuff, the only item of furniture was an old roll-top desk against one wall. Michael picked his way through the debris on the floor and shifted a couple of armfuls of books and stationery, so that an empty space was left on the desktop.

"It's all yours," he said with a slight smile. "If you need any help with homework, give us a yell."

"Thanks," Arkie mumbled, settling herself on the ancient revolving office chair that was parked next to the desk. She sat back and pushed the chair so that it swung right around in a sweeping view of the small, cluttered room. Michael had pulled the door closed, and she could hear his voice, distantly in the kitchen. Above her there were muffled thumps as Ian and Jo continued their games with toy cars, and outside the breeze sent the garden bushes scraping against the glass of the window. Arkie pulled schoolbooks, pen and ruler from her bag, and set to work.

In the relative isolation the room afforded, she felt her anger gradually subside. She began working steadily. *I should have asked about this room before.* She'd not really ventured in here very much, except to collect the vacuum cleaner every once in a while. Mum and Michael didn't actually use it either; their schoolwork was mostly completed at the tables in the kitchen or lounge-room — close to the coffee and tea.

Arkie heard the workmen's vehicles next door start up and leave, and the sky outside gradually dimmed into twilight. Michael, Jo and Ian walked up the side path then, with Headley anxiously straining at his lead, eager for the walk. Out in the kitchen the radio echoed softly and bowls and saucepans were rattled as mum started getting the evening meal together. Arkie laboured over a title page in her social science book, interrupting her artistic efforts only to switch on the light as darkness filled the room.

There were footsteps on the path outside, a conversation between Michael and Jo and the rattle of Headley's collar and lead as they returned. Ian did not seem to be with them. The homework nearly completed, Arkie began more and more to look about the room. Its clutter interested her, and she began to pick out the readily visible things — dog-eared high school copies of *Far From The Madding Crowd* and *Brave New World*, stencilled sheets that were stacked in a plastic tote tray on the floor, a thick blue folder on one bookshelf labelled *Susan Gerhardt Secondary Music*, and a grease-marked and well-used book, *Holden FX-FJ Workshop Manual*, that obviously belonged to Michael's rusty utility.

The roll-top desk had several drawers, which she began to open in turn. The first yielded an assortment of stationery, paper and small batteries of various shapes. The next few drawers contained more sheets of paper and manila folders. There were also, Arkie noted with growing curiosity, envelopes of photographs. The bottom drawer was larger than the rest, and when she opened it two items commanded her attention. The first was a large, faded colour photograph, a group portrait of thirty or more children who were standing or seated in tidy rows against the backdrop of a park or large garden. They were all holding musical instruments — flutes, violins, trombones, cellos, oboes — and were all dressed in white T-shirts and red shorts or dresses. Although Arkie scanned the rows of faces twice over, there was no sight of her mum, who seemed at that moment to be the obvious connection with the photograph. Puzzled, Arkie replaced the picture in the drawer.

It's like a school photo or something, except there's nothing written on the back. No names, nothing.

The second item she lifted from the drawer was a leather carry case containing a heavy old camera. *Voigtlander* was embossed in scrolled lettering on the camera's top, and once Arkie had released an obvious looking catch, the lens revealed itself, outstretched at the end of a leather concertina. *A real antique*, she thought, fascinated, and examined the contraption from every angle. There were numerical adjustments and catches everywhere.

"How's the homework?"

Startled, she folded the camera back into its case. Michael had leant against the doorway to ask his question, but now made his way over to the desk. "Just finished," Arkie said with a shrug, trying to remain collected. She held the maths stencil and social science exercise book for him to look at. "It was good working in here," she added.

With a slight laugh, Michael said, "And what amazing things have you been discovering in this rubbish tip of a room?"

"I was curious," she answered, meaning it as an apology, because the bottom drawer was still open.

"Uh huh."

Arkie folded her stencil, closed the workbook and collected her textas and pencils. She glanced at Michael, unable to work out the expression on his face, caught as he was between a contemplative smile and a hint of solemnity. He seemed to be looking over at the bookshelves.

"I found this photo and camera," she said quickly, pulling the photo out again. "D' you know where this photo comes from? Who are all these kids?"

Michael knelt down and ran a finger along the front row of children, the youngest in the group. "That's me," he said, pointing.

Arkie gaped, looked closer. The Michael in the photograph was half-kneeling, half-standing, as if poised to run, and his chin jutted out, oddly proud. He had a mop of blond, curling hair, and a distant, unsmiling expression to his face. In one hand, he held a violin and bow. She looked at the Michael who knelt beside her, who had a thin, chiselled face and a receding hairline. "That's you?" she said, deeply surprised. "Really?"

Michael nodded. "Sure is."

"I didn't know you knew how to play the violin."

"I did, once."

"Why don't you play now?"

"I got tired of it. Gave it away."

"Why?"

"I just did."

It was the first time she had ever seen a picture of Michael as a child. "Where was the photo taken?"

"School holiday camp. A retreat for musically inclined children, somewhere in the Dandenongs. I can't quite remember where."

"Can I borrow it?"

"What, this photo?"

"Yeah. For the Atrocity Cabinet. Because it's interesting."

Michael paused. "No," he said firmly but gently, taking it from Arkie's grasp and replacing it in the drawer. He pulled the camera out. "This was my dad's," he went on. "He bought it second-hand, so who knows how old it might be. I haven't used it for years; your mum seems to be the photographer around here." He clicked the case open and unfolded the lens. "It takes good photos. D' you have a camera, still?"

"That instamatic I got when I was six. Except it's full of sand and I don't think it works any more."

"Hmm," Michael considered, closing the camera up and handing it to Arkie. "In that case, have this."

"Have it?"

"Keep it. If you'd like it, that is."

Arkie nodded.

"I'll show you how to work it, as long as you

show me how the first roll of pictures turn out."
He pushed the desk's bottom drawer closed.
"Agreed?"

"Agreed," Arkie replied, smiling, "Thanks,
Michael."

He stood up and walked back to the doorway.
"A pleasure. It'll be nice to see it in use after all
this time."

"Oi!" mum's voice rang out from the loungeroom, "Arkie! Have you finished that homework
yet?"

"Yes!"

"Great!" mum called back. "I can make some
noise before dinner."

There was a burst of piano then, erratic warm-
up notes at first, and then a rumbling blues beat
with mum's seldom-heard, gravelly voice to
match.

"Back in the U.S. — back in the U.S.S.R.,"
came Jo's reedy voice as well, because he'd heard
mum play this particular song before, and he
knew all the words.

FOUR

She could see her reflection in the mirror of Jo's wardrobe as she backed away towards the blank wall beside her bed. *There's that picture of a Russian peasant girl in one of the* National Geographics *at school, and that's who I look like.* The thought pleased Arkie, and she smiled crookedly, just as the camera clicked.

After Michael had shown her how to load the roll of back-and-white film, he'd told her how to set the self-timing control, so that she could include herself in photographs. So now, the camera had been sat on the chair, which in turn was on top of the work table in her bedroom and pointed at where she stood against the bare wall.

Rats. I didn't mean to smile.

She walked over, wound the film on, and set the timer again, before darting back to her position. Her footsteps made Jo's wardrobe mirror vibrate, and she could see her reflection again, her cropped mouse-brown hair, black dress and tights and white ballet shoes.

The camera clicked again.

She packed it away then, onto a shelf in the Atrocity Cabinet, alongside the blithely smiling Barbie doll with its missing leg. She clattered the chair back onto the floor, and sat down at the work table. Jo and Ian were outside in the garden, whooping around after the dog, and next door some kids from school were weaving their bikes around the maze of newly bricked foundations that occupied the centre of the formerly vacant block. The screen door downstairs creaked open and slammed shut as Jo bounded inside, about the same time as Mum and Michael arrived home in the Batmobile.

Jo came into the bedroom. "Aw, Arkie! Why'd you put all this over here?" he complained. Comics, colouring in books and crayons were heaped on his bed. He knelt down and scooped up his soccer ball.

"It was on the table, and I needed the table."

"But I was using these!" he said accusingly. "Why'd you mess them up?"

"Because I had work to do and I needed the table, for crying out loud! And YOU were outside. You weren't even up here!"

Jo picked up a handful of books and crayons and stalked over to the work table. "You always touch my things and move them around and hide them and tell me it's my fault for not being able to find them."

"What's got into you?" Arkie asked in amazement, "All I did —"

"You think you're smart, Arkie. One day, I'm

49

going to hide your textas and school things somewhere. Then you'll know what it's like having people mess around with your things."

Downstairs, the front door opened. "Are you two fighting up there?" came mum's voice.

"No!" Arkie called.

"Yes!" shouted Jo.

"We could hear you from outside," mum continued. "What's going on?"

Jo dumped his handful of things back on the table. "Leave my stuff alone," he hissed.

"Buzz off, Jo."

"Buzz off yourself!"

"Go away and play, little boy."

"D' you want me to rip your homework up?"

"D' you want a thump in the head?"

"D' you want me to tell mum you once stabbed me in the leg?"

Arkie paused. She had done that, months before. She'd been practising throwing her new pocket knife at a specially marked target on the laundry wall, when Jo had seemed to get himself in the way. When he'd started howling blue murder, and threatening to tell mum and Michael, Arkie had devised her only ever attempt at bribery.

"Jo, I'll give you a whole dollar if you don't tell."

"Not likely!" he'd sobbed back, as blood dribbled from the puncture mark below his knee, "Look at what you done. I'm telling."

"Two dollars, then."

"Alright, I won't tell."

Two dollars had been a small fortune to Arkie at the time, and must have kept Jo in red ice blocks for nearly a week. But it had sure beaten having the pocket knife confiscated and going through an inquisition with mum and probably Michael as well.

She snapped back to the present. "You'd better not tell her about that."

"I will. And I am." He made for the door.

"Little dobber. You wait, Jo."

"You'd better not touch me. I've already got scars from you."

"You wait till I see the kids from your class at school tomorrow. Wait till you hear what I tell them."

"What'll you tell them?"

"That you still wet the bed." *Why did I say that?*

"You'd better not!"

"And that you hide behind a pillow when there's scary bits on 'Dr Who'."

"Aw, Arkie! You'd better not!"

Out in the yard she could see Ian, patiently waiting for Jo's return, and she hesitated as Jo stormed back across the room and collapsed in a sullen and defeated heap on the end of his bed.

Why did I say that? Kylie would say something like that.

"You're a rat, Arkie," Jo mumbled.

Mum's footsteps were on the stairs. "What's going on?"

"Nothing," Arkie replied quietly.

"She moved my stuff off the work table and didn't put it back," Jo replied.

Mum clicked her tongue in annoyance, and looked mildly harassed. "Look, I'm getting really tired of this fighting. Arkie, put his things back where you found them next time. Jo, if you're playing a game with Ian, you'd better get a move on. It'll be dark before too long."

Jo left the room in nose-wrinkled silence.

"Mum . . ." Arkie started to say.

"Yes?"

"I was going to put his stuff back."

Her mum nodded. "Alright, alright, it's over and done with. Any homework tonight?"

"I'll do it after dinner. Can I go down to Kylie's for a while?"

"Mmm, be home by six, though."

"Okay. Thanks."

Michael was in the loungeroom putting a record onto the stereo turntable. "Have a good day?" he asked.

"Apart from just now," Arkie answered as she headed for the front door.

Michael grinned. "That's life, eh?"

"I tried out the self-timing control on the camera this afternoon," she added, and stepped outside. A rush of recorded music followed.

The workmen next door had packed up and left early that day, and the kids from school were still hanging around.

"Hey, Arkie!" one of them called from amongst the piles of bricks, dirt and rubble, "Ark,

Ark!" His voice sounded like a car horn.

"In your nose with a rubber hose!" she called back, and gave a finger signal to match.

"Ark Ark!" he called out again, as she jogged down the steep part of the hill towards the ranks of home units.

Where Kylie lived was most of the way back toward the shopping centre and the main road; a dark brick building with a landscaped garden of native shrubs trapped amongst cemented bush-rock. There was a group of litte kids hanging aound the entrance doorway, and when Arkie climbed the carpeted staircase she heard the usual mixture of sounds from behind each numbered door — adult and child voices, televisions, stereos, cool silence.

I hope Rebecca isn't here.

But as it turned out, Kylie had just closed the door of unit twelve behind her, and met Arkie in the hall.

"I've gotta return these videos for mum," she said, pocketing a door key with one hand, and clutching two plastic video cases with the other. "Want t' come down the shops?"

Arkie nodded.

"Why are you dressed in that?" Kylie said, pointing. "Y' look like you're going to a funeral. Black — yuk."

"What's wrong with it?"

"You look daggy."

"What's daggy about it? It's what I felt like wearing, that's all."

"Jeez, you're weird, Arkie," Kylie commented,

not quite sneeringly, and then added quickly, "How come you came down, anyway? You don't visit after school as much as you used to."

"I didn't feel like doing homework. And Jo was being a pest, so I thought —"

"You're always doing homework. Or reading books or something."

On the street, a lazy, informal game of football had begun. Sean Taylor, Adam Black and half a dozen other kids had ranged themselves across the bitumen.

Sean Taylor yelled out, "Hey, Arkie, you're going the wrong way! Adam's over here!"

"We're coming back!" Kylie replied obligingly.

Arkie frowned and kept walking. "Cut it out, Kylie," she muttered.

"Come on, what's wrong? Adam's alright."

"He's a pain."

"Hey, you danced with him at the last school disco —"

"He just barged up and starting dancing. I didn't even ask him. Anyway, you danced with Mr Clifton, and no-one's been matching you up with him. So stop matching me up with Adam Black. Urk."

Peak-hour traffic had started to filter north-ward from the city, and public buses squealed to a halt at the bus stop, disgorging office workers and children from private schools. Clearly visible on the bus stop seat was *Arkie G. loves* written in texta, with a dash of scribble at the end where the texta had been wrestled from Sean Taylor's grasp.

"You're famous," Kylie said as they passed it by, but Arkie ignored her.

She waited, almost impatiently, as Kylie roamed along the stacked shelves in the video hire shop. It was actually part of the local service station, vacant space at one end of the spare parts section that was now lined with movie cassette boxes. From the adjacent car work bay echoed the clatter of a spanner being dropped on the cement floor, and sporadic talk between the mechanics.

"What d' you reckon about that 4:1 diff, Evan?"

"Well, if you've got it hooked up to a. . . ."

Michael sometimes wandered down at weekends to talk about old cars with the mechanics, who, it seemed to Arkie, lived at the service station. They spent entire Saturdays and Sundays with their own cars wheeled over the service pits, amid constant conversations about wheels, paint jobs and engines.

Kylie was still surveying what was available on the video shelves.

"How many of these d' you get each week?" she asked.

"Mum and Michael only let us watch one video a week."

"One? Wow, no wonder there's nothing to do at your place."

It had seemed a long time since Arkie had been inside where Kylie lived, and she was surprised by the emptiness and quiet of unit twelve when they returned.

"Mum's working new shifts now," Kylie said, dumping two newly hired video tapes on the couch and automatically switching the TV on. "She doesn't get home from the office until six-thirty."

The centre of Kylie's loungeroom was occupied by a full laundry basket. "All mine," Kylie went on. "Mum said to iron it all by tonight, but I don't think I will —" She gazed at the TV for a moment and then briskly changed channels. "Boring stuff," she mumbled, and switched the set off.

Arkie had already seated herself on one of the leather armchairs, expecting her visit to consist of watching television, and was surprised when Kylie walked over instead to the balcony door and slid it open.

"Come and sit out here and we can perve on everybody," she said.

Two cane chairs jostled for space on the cement balcony, and the view through the iron railings was of street, cars and other units.

"These plants aren't doing too well," Kylie remarked. "Mum says it's all the fumes from the traffic."

"The plants at our place do okay."

"It always smells around here. Cars and trucks, other people's garbage."

"The sea smells nice. At night, when there's a breeze, I can smell the salt air from my bedroom."

"Yuk, you're kidding. All the sea smells of is dead seaweed."

Arkie shrugged. "Sometimes, I guess."

"All the time," Kylie stated emphatically. "And when mum cleans the windows here, all this black muck from car exhausts comes off. Sometimes I can't stand this place."

From the balcony there was a view of the

beach and ocean, and when Arkie glanced in the other direction, her own house was visible beyond the other blocks of home units and the vacant block.

"That's a try!" came shouts from the street as the game of football continued.

"I remember when you first moved here and started at school," Kylie said abruptly. "We were six and had that teacher —"

"— Mrs Handly."

"— yeah, Mrs Handly, and she made you sit next to me. You were really quiet and didn't talk to anyone for ages."

"It was a bit scary starting at a new school, you know," Arkie said, trying not to sound defensive. "I missed my other school, anyway. I had a really nice teacher, except I can't remember her name."

Kylie looked away, and absently began to chew a fingernail.

"I didn't miss the flat we lived in, but," Arkie added.

"What? How come?"

"It was really cramped. Mum, my dad and me, then Jo as well. Every time I wanted to play outside, mum had to come out with me."

"Why?"

"It was right on a busy road. Cars, strangers, all that stuff. I didn't like living there. It was good when we moved in with Michael."

"But that place is ancient," Kylie remarked disapprovingly." All those cobwebs under the house, pieces of timber and car bits."

Arkie rolled her eyes. "We don't live under the house, do we?"

"No, I didn't mean that —"

"It's great inside, and that's what counts."

Kylie shrugged, closely inspecting her fingers. Down on the street an older girl in an elaborate school uniform and carrying a briefcase, walked slowly along the footpath. Her head was lowered in silent contemplation, and she appeared oblivious to the noisy game of street football, and to everything else around.

"Wow," Kylie said quietly so that only Arkie could have heard, "I couldn't handle wearing something like that every school day — gloves, hat and stockings." Then she added, without any jocularity, "My mum might be sending me to a private high school. Catholic girls' college or something —"

"Yeah?"

"— I told her I don't want to, but . . ."

"I'm going to where mum and Michael teach," Arkie said with some relief. "Most of the kids are going there."

"Well, it's the closest high school to here, isn't it?" Kylie replied antagonistically. She undid one of her hairclips and rearranged her blonde tresses.

"Your hair looks good like that," Arkie told her.

"Like this?" Kylie asked, holding up a handful of chest-length hair. "It's because I've been plaiting it at night and undoing the plaits before school each day."

"I used to do that."

"Yeah, but you went and had your hair cut, didn't you? How come? You never told me why."

"I just felt like it. Mum let me."

"My mum wouldn't have. We used to almost look the same, you and I. Same length hair, same height —"

"Our eyes are the same colour."

"You're still as skinny as a rake."

"You've got more freckles than me."

"Just on my nose. And you can hardly see them."

The brief, speeding conversation ground to a halt, and the two of them stared at each other for a moment. Kylie looked away first, and it was to point at something across the road.

"See that window over there?" she said, pointing at a block of cream brick home units directly opposite. "The one with the butterfly curtains? That's Rebecca's bedroom." She glanced sideways at Arkie, and added, "She goes to yoga classes after school every Thursday; that's why she's not around at the moment."

"My mum goes to yoga classes Wednesday nights," Arkie said, but Kylie didn't acknowledge this.

"We've got this signal system going," Kylie continued with mounting enthusiasm. "It's great. We use our bedroom lights and the venetian blinds on our windows, like Morse code or something. It's good fun."

Arkie nodded, and didn't feel jealous. Just adrift, as though she was letting go of something that would have fended her off regardless.

59

"Rebecca and me are probably going roller skating this weekend," Kylie added as a parting shot.

Jo and Ian were playing in the dusk light outside, chasing the soccer ball around the backyard, when Arkie came home. Headley was growling after the ball too and there were two boys from Jo's class at school, as well as Michael, who sent the ball skating back into the playing area whenever it came too close to where he was watering the garden.

"Wanna play, Arkie?" Jo called to her.

She shook her head, but stopped at the back steps for a moment. From inside the house came sporadic bursts of music and synthetic percussion; mum doodling at her piano and synthesizer.

"Come on, Arkie!" Jo called again. "You're good at soccer."

But again, she shook her head. The boys squealed and yelled after the ball, until it veered back to where Michael stood at the vegetable garden. He glared at them in mock anger, set the hose down on the ground and picked the ball up. Automatically, the boys scattered to the corners of the yard — under the rickety pergola and the trees at the far fence, as Jo said breathlessly and loudly, "Michael can kick a ball across a whole soccer field!"

Michael slowly and deliberately kicked the ball to Ian, who moved apprehensively and missed it altogether. Jo laughed goodnaturedly, but the other two boys shouted fearless insults and howled derisively.

Michael frowned and said, "Hey, come on, you guys. Everyone's entitled to miss sometimes."

Ian picked up the ball and kicked it to no-one in particular. Arkie climbed the back steps and went inside.

Her mum was seated at the piano, staring at the keyboard. Through the amplifier that lay on the floor next to the piano came the rattle and thump of percussion, until mum reached beside her and flicked a switch on the synthesizer. The sound ceased, and mum said with a grimace, "I'm not feeling particularly inspired today."

Arkie walked up and squeezed herself onto the piano stool next to her. "Why not?"

"I can't compose on an empty stomach."

"Well, have something to eat, then."

"I'm conserving my hunger. It's pay day today; we're going out for a meal."

"Great! Chinese or Moroccan?"

"Moroccan."

"Jo keeps asking about going to McDonalds —"

"Huh!" mum said with a laugh. "Jo can think again! How was Kylie?"

"Alright, I guess."

"Haven't seen much of her these past few months."

Arkie shrugged. "She's always busy or going out somewhere..."

"Hmm."

"Can I use the spare room to do some homework? Before we go out?"

"You've got your own bedroom to yourself at the moment."

"Jo'll be inside soon. Please." She blinked her eyes and put on her Barbie doll grin.

Mum pulled a face. "Go on, then. If there's any stuff on the desk, put it over on the bookshelf, or something." She added, "You look like a Barbie doll when you pull faces like that, Arkie."

Arkie returned downstairs with her school-bag. "Play something, mum," she called from inside the spare room.

"Like what?" mum called back.

"Anything. Some of your own music."

The piano tinkled into life. "This isn't one of mine," mum said. "It's by a composer called Debussy. I learnt it when I was a little bit older than you."

The spare room looked exactly as it had a few days beforehand, a maze of boxes and para-phernalia. Feeling pleased, Arkie settled herself at the roll-top desk and emptied the contents of her schoolbag.

Maths and spelling, my very favourites. Yuk.

The music in the loungeroom dipped, rose and flowed on.

There were calls of goodbye and footsteps outside, as the visiting boys left for home. Shortly after came the sound of another set of footsteps as Ian left also.

What are you having for dinner, Ian?

Michael's and Jo's voices were in the kitchen, talking about soccer, and the piano music ceased. Arkie stood up, turned the light on and pushed the door closed. In the loungeroom the TV was switched on, and a newsreader's voice spoke at low volume.

The heaters weren't on at school this morning. We all froze to death at our desks, and Mr Clifton kept his scarf and gloves on.

Arkie slid the bottom drawer open, and picked the colour photograph out to look at. Michael's child face stared back at her, distantly.

I can tell it's you, Michael, by your eyes. She held the photo closely, and then at a distance. *You look sad.*

Frowning thoughtfully, she put the photo back in its drawer. Homework sat unfinished on the desk, but she swung herself slowly around on the old office chair so that her gaze took in the entire room with its shelves and boxes of rubbish and treasure.

I like this room.

At the table in the crowded, warm restaurant, Arkie asked, "How old is our house?"

"It was built in the nineteen-twenties," Michael answered, "probably as somone's week-ender, because in those days it would have been a whole morning's drive from Sydney. No Harbour Bridge, then. And the house would have been surrounded by bushland. No home units."

Arkie nodded. She had once tried hunting for clues of the house's history and of previous tenants, but without much success. In the concrete path, down towards what had once been the outdoor dunny, there was BRIAN 12.8.42, scratched in assertive capital letters. In the bathroom upstairs, the paint on the wall around the tub had peeled away to reveal half a dozen previous colours. When mum or Michael dug the garden, they often sifted up old nails, bits of china (always *bits*) and other nondescript shapes, rusted away. A few of the artefacts wound up in Arkie's Atrocity Cabinet.

"What was it like when you first lived there, but?"

"What was it like?" mum grinned, guessing wildly. "Loud parties, Michael sleeping in until twelve every day, rubbish bins overflowing with beer cans. That's what I reckon it was like!" She laughed, and her dangling earrings danced and rattled.

"It wasn't like that at all!" Michael protested. "Don't believe a word of it, Arkie. The house was exactly as it is now. The street was a little bit different. Where that Spanish villa thing is, across the road from us, there used to be another weatherboard weekender. And next door to where Kylie lives, there was another house. They were both demolished, and I guess there were other houses that have been demolished over the years."

"Will we get demolished?" Jo asked. He had gradually worked his way through a bowl of black olives that had been set on the table as an entree for the four of them.

"I sure hope not," Michael said with a sigh.

"It's a bummer about that vacant block being built on, but with luck we'll be left neighbourless for a while, yet."

The restaurant was fifteen minutes' walk from home, a converted shop in a tiny side street between the main road and the beach.

"It used to be a milkbar," Michael told them once, "a real surfie dive — cans of coke, a dirty lino floor, a deafening jukebox."

Someone in the kitchen had classical music playing on a tape deck, and the aroma of spicy food filled the room where tables of people joked and conversed. The restaurant's patterned walls were handpainted. One was in tones of geometric green and brown. The wall facing that had swirling, organic shapes in softer shades of blue and grey. On each was a band of strong colour that wove its way endlessly, exactly, through the entire pattern. As he often did, Jo was sitting in his chair, weaving his face and eyes groggily about, trying to follow the painted lines through their complicated journeys across each wall.

"Stop it!" Michael said to Jo, pulling a face of mock horror. "It makes me dizzy just looking at you."

"I can't. . .I can't. . ." Jo droned, determined to follow the line back to its starting point.

"I like pay days," mum said, as plates of food were brought to their table.

I have to ask about the room.

"It was funny this afternoon," Jo said in between mouthfuls, "when Ian missed the ball, he almost fell over backwards."

"I got a bit annoyed with those two other friends of yours," Michael said.

"Duane and Paul?"

"Mmm," Michael continued, oddly stern. "I hope you don't carry on like they did whenever someone can't do something too well."

"Not me," Jo responded. "Ian's my best friend. I wouldn't make fun of him."

"Who was your best friend at school, Michael?" Arkie asked.

Michael looked taken aback. He glanced about vaguely, and said, "I dunno, really...I don't even have any idea what all the kids from school are doing these days. I haven't been back to Melbourne for a long time." He resumed eating and made no further reply. *That wasn't an answer.* She switched her gaze to her mum. *Who's your best friend, mum?*

"Carol," mum said suddenly. "I haven't seen her for ages. Two years I think. Before she and John moved onto the farm. The baby must be quite a few months old, now. We got that photo in the mail in April."

"Who?" Jo asked.

"Carol. She came to visit us ages ago, driving that dinged-up station wagon held together with bumper stickers."

"I remember," Jo said. "The lady with the old-fashioned glasses —"

"Horn-rimmed," Arkie interrupted. *I have to ask about the room.*

"We must go and visit them," mum said with emphasis, half to herself. "I keep putting it off.

66

That's what we have to do next school holidays —
what d' you think, Mike?"

Michael shrugged. "Suits me fine."

"How long have you known Carol?" Arkie
asked, knowing that there were photos in one of
the albums at home of mum and Carol in starchy
school uniforms, clasping tennis racquets and
grinning wickedly.

"Oh. . ." mum replied, hurrying through a
mouthful of food, "since we were twelve. When I
started boarding school, I met Carol. I probably
wouldn't have lasted the next six years,
otherwise."

*My best friend for a whole year in kindergarten
was Julieann Vernon, but then I changed schools.
Mrs Handly sat me next to Kylie.*

Ask now.

"You know the spare room?" she said. "Can I
have that as my bedroom?"

Mum, Michael and Jo all looked at her. Mum
said, not without surprise, "Are you serious?"

"Uh huh. Yes."

"It's full of stuff Arkie, and it's not very big."

"It's big enough for me."

"Where are we going to put everything?" mum
asked.

"I dunno," Arkie said.

"That school stuff needs sorting out anyway,"
Michael said to mum. "All of it, plus the bookshelves, would fit into our room upstairs."

Mum nodded and sighed. "What's wrong with
your own room?"

"I'm sick of sharing. I need some space," Arkie

replied. When she looked at Jo, he lowered his face and looked apprehensive, so she added, "It's not fair on Jo, either. He'd probably like more space to play, and to have his toys and things."

"That upstairs bedroom has a great view," mum continued, nonplussed, "which is why we let you and Jo have it. There's not much of a view from the spare room, apart from the garden." She paused. "Do you really want to change rooms?"

Arkie nodded. "Can I?"

Mum looked at Michael, who shrugged and said, "Fine with me."

Outside in the night, a blue-and-white city bus carried a sprinkling of late workers on to their respective bus stops. The shopfront windows were captured brilliantly by their own night lighting and by the illumination of the streetlamps. A brisk, salt breeze blew up from the ocean, and mum, Michael, Arkie and Jo walked home in the cool.

"We should've driven to the restaurant," Jo mumbled, and jogged on ahead, his nylon jacket flapping and rustling.

The traffic banked up as they crossed at the traffic lights; carloads of people on their way home from late-night shopping in the city.

"Wait for us," mum called to Jo as he sprinted along the footpath, past the takeaway and milkbar.

I've got my own bedroom. Great.

"Can I move into the spare room tonight?" Arkie asked.

"Some people are keen!" Michael exclaimed, and tried tickling her under the arms.

"Well?" Arkie struggled free, laughing. "Can I?"

"We will clear a space," mum said in a resigned voice, "in the middle of the floor in the spare room, we will drag your mattress downstairs, and you can spend tonight in your new room — satisfied?"

"Yep," Arkie grinned.

A group of high school kids sprawled and lounged at laminex tables inside the takeaway. One of them called out to Michael, "Hey sir, is that your family?"

Michael raised his eyebrows and nodded.

There was the usual clatter and hum of conversation from inside the Parade Hotel. As they passed by, Arkie caught the vacant gazes of the elderly regulars seated behind the glass of the footpath windows. The tables and chairs behind them were crowded with laughing, animated drinkers, and the jukebox in one far corner was rasping and rumbling with music. An elderly man sat alone at the bar, curled over on his seat and clutching a half-empty glass, as a barmaid wiped the counter down wearily in between attending to customers.

Michael and mum walked on ahead, around the corner into Ramsay Street, and then Arkie heard Michael say, "Hullo Ian."

Ian was sitting on the pub steps. He was rugged up in jumper and jacket, and clutching a white paper package. Jo had sat down next to him. "Hullo," Ian replied, through a mouthful of chips.

"Is your mum inside?" Michael asked.

Ian nodded. "She won't let me have the key any more, because last time I went home and fell asleep and didn't hear her banging on the door when she came home."

Michael sighed.

Mum said, "Do you want to come back up to our place for a while, have some supper? A cup of milo and something to eat?"

Ian nodded. "I'll have to . . ."

"Duck inside and tell your mum where you are," mum added.

Ian reappeared a minute or so later.

"Did she say okay?" Michael asked.

"I think so —" Ian said with a shrug.

"Well, come on then," mum said, resting a hand briefly on his shoulder and then starting off along the footpath.

Arkie walked, head down, past the rubbish bins, parked cars and home units of Ramsay Street. *I wish I'd had my camera with me just then. I would've taken a photo back at those hotel steps.*

70

FIVE

Jo was perched on Michael's back, and hanging on for grim life.

"G'night, Arkie," he said, leaning over.

"Urk, Jo, that wasn't a kiss, it was a dribble. Good night."

Mum was snuggled up on the lounge watching a television documentary.

"G'night, mum."

"Night, little one. Sweet dreams, stay dry."

"Yeah," Jo answered with a mandatory sigh, and then commanded to Michael, "Upstairs, captain!" Jo was enjoying his sole possession of the bedroom. The novelty hadn't worn off, after more than a week.

Michael paused at the staircase. "Arkie, are you coming up to hear the rest of the story? It's the last chapter."

"No thanks," Arkie replied.

"You sure?"

"I'm sure," she said, settling on the lounge next to mum.

"Okay," Michael called, piggybacking Jo upstairs.

"No more bedtime stories, huh?" mum commented.

"I'll read it myself in the morning," Arkie said, quietly obstinate.

She could hear muffled conversation upstairs, and then Michael's expressive voice leading Jo through the closing paragraphs of a C. S. Lewis fantasy.

The first night we arrived here, Michael read to me. I didn't even look at the pictures in the book or anything, just stared and stared at Michael. My dad never read me anything. The removal van brought our things from the flat, and the loungeroom here was full of boxes and extra furniture. Mum couldn't get Jo to sleep in his cot in the upstairs bedroom and he cried half the night.

In the morning when Arkie woke, the first thing that caught her eye was the C. S. Lewis book, mysteriously deposited on the top of the roll-top desk.

"Thanks, Michael," she murmured to herself, and gazed about the rest of the room, at all of her possessions from upstairs that had gradually been shifted down — her wardrobe, the Atrocity Cabinet, the chest of drawers, her books in teetering piles on the floor next to the desk.

"I'll clean the rest of my stuff out soon," Michael kept promising. The pine bookshelves and all the school things had gone into mum's and Michael's room, the pushbike and cot had migrated under the house. An old tapestry couch from upstairs had found its way to the space beneath the window, and was now catching fragments of early morning sunlight. The contents of the desk had not been moved.

Mum's initial scepticism had shifted. "There's hardly room to move in here," she said, "but I tell you what, when the weather warms up some more, we'll paint the room out for you. You can choose the colour, if you want."

Rugged up in her quilt, Arkie curled up on the couch beneath her bedroom window, and finished reading C. S. Lewis. The silence that had filled the house as sunlight outside shifted layers of fog was broken by the sound of footsteps upstairs.

When she heard Michael say loudly, "Hooray! Dry pyjamas!" she decided that Jo had woken and wandered into the main bedroom. At this point the upstairs noise increased — jokey talk between mum and Michael and squealing from Jo, because someone was tickling him. Arkie maintained concentration on C. S. Lewis until she'd finished the story, and then got up and walked out into the kitchen. She filled the kettle with water and switched it on, then opened the back door for Goodvibes to come in, because he'd spent the night outdoors on the prowl.

"Come here, pig," she mumbled, setting a saucer of milk down for him.

Upstairs, Jo was yelling, "Agh, stop it, stop it!"

Armed with her camera, Arkie padded upstairs, pausing outside the bedroom door to spring the lens open and adjust the light setting.

"You're the most ticklish kid I've ever met," Michael was saying to Jo. "Must be because you take after your mum."

There was a burst of giggles from mum then,

just as Arkie stepped into the doorway. "Smile, everyone," she announced in a deadpan voice, clicking the camera. Its view had found their laughing faces and dishevelled hair; Jo burrowed between mum and Michael in the double bed.

"Oh no!" mum said, hiding her face behind the sheets too late. Then she resurfaced, saying, "give me that camera! I want to take one of you, Arkie, in your puppy-dog slippers and that daggy dressing gown. C'mon!"

"No way!" Arkie laughed.

"How's life downstairs treating you, then?" Michael asked.

"Fine," Arkie replied. "Does anyone want tea of coffee?"

"Oooh, room service," mum said in a tone of mock surprise. "I love these people who wake up early. Tea, please."

"Same, please," answered Michael. "Great service in this hotel. I might stay another year —"

Mum reached over and tried to tickle him.

"I'll have coffee," Jo called from under the blankets.

"Get it yourself," Arkie told him. "I'm talking to the old folks, not to you."

"Which old folks are you talking about?" mum demanded.

"These ones in here," Arkie said, backing out the door. "Two high school teachers. Over the hill, they are."

Mum pulled a face and Michael said, "We need our rest. What about those cups of tea?"

"I'll send you the bill," Arkie remarked dryly, as she went downstairs.

"What about a coffee?" Jo called after her. "And vegemite on toast?"

"Fat chance," Arkie called back. Jo was giggling once more, but then there was the thump of something — or someone — landing on the floor, and the giggles turned to a wail and sobs. "Ha ha!" Arkie said from the kitchen, loud enough to be heard. When she returned with two mugs of tea, Jo was on the carpet beside the bed, sniffling to himself.

"What happened to you?" Arkie asked.

"He kind of...rolled out of bed," Michael grimaced, leaning over and attempting to pick Jo up by his pyjama pants. "Come on, you're not dead yet."

"Almost," sniffed Jo, who then dissolved into more giggles.

Arkie shook her head at Jo. "You're loopy, mate." Then she asked, "Can I go and get the papers?"

"Sure," mum said, between sips of tea, "there's money on top of the fridge."

"Can I go too?" Jo whined.

"No," said mum with surprising bluntness, "leave your sister in peace. You spent half of last weekend down the shops with Ian, wasting pocket money on those computer games..."

Arkie speedily changed into daytime clothes, pocketed the spare change from on top of the fridge, and stepped outside. As an afterthought, she traipsed around the back, put Headley onto his walking leash and set off with him heaving and straining at the lead.

"Anyone'd think we never exercise you," she

grumbled, straining to keep herself at a walking pace and not go toppling over as she negotiated the steep section of road between the house and the blocks of home units. Joggers were out and about in their tracksuits, springing along the footpaths on either side of the main road. Their running shoes tapped and clunked on the cement in an almost military rhythm, and their heaving breath misted in the cold morning air. A couple of high school boys clasping waxed surfboards waited at the pedestrian crossing next to the lights, casting anxious anticipatory gazes at the waves kicking and spilling onto the nearby beach.

They're kidding; the water'll be freezing. The municipal pool's bad enough, and it's heated.

Arkie didn't stay long at the newsagent; just long enough to browse through a *Dolly* magazine and a *Vogue* she couldn't afford, before grabbing the Sunday papers and clattering the money for them onto the counter.

When she returned to the house, Ian was standing at the front door, dressed in jeans and crumpled sweater, looking dishevelled and only just awake.

"Didn't you knock?" Arkie asked, pushing the door open.

"Mmm," he answered, "but no-one heard."

"Should have knocked louder," she said in reply, "they're all still upstairs in bed. It's early, Ian."

"I know," he said quietly, and then pointed at the lead in Arkie's hand. "Can I take Headley back to his kennel?"

She nodded and passed the lead to Ian's

waiting clasp. He led Headley back down the steps and into the yard where he stopped for a moment.

"Headley, Headley!" he said in a bright voice, dropping the lead and holding a hand high in the air, so that Headley began to spring up in frantic, enthusiastic leaps. Ian laughed and backed away towards the rear of the house. "Come on, up, up!"

"Stop that, Ian!" Arkie shouted sharply, so that Ian froze and looked at her with his mouth open. "We've been trying to teach the dog not t' do that, and now I know where he's learnt it from." She went to add something more in an irritated voice, but Ian looked so crestfallen that Arkie instead told him, "The back door's open. You can come into the kitchen and get Headley some breakfast. Make sure he's on his chain first, but."

Sometimes it's like I've got two little brothers instead of one.

"You should've seen all the cockroaches I zapped with the spray yesterday," Jo told Ian breathlessly. "There were hundreds under the sink!"

Ian laughed quietly. "I found a cockroach in a cereal packet, once."

Michael pulled a face of extreme horror, grabbed the Weetbix packet from the table, and rustled through its contents. Both boys giggled.

From the stereo in the loungeroom came muted hilarity and music, as the FM radio announcer hammed it up between songs. Arkie leaned her elbow on the table, thoughtfully chewing honey and toast and watching the sunlight stream through the loungeroom windows, filtering colourfully through the glass windchimes that hung above the bookshelves.

"You know what there is for breakfast," mum had told Ian, "just help yourself." And Ian had, almost as if he'd lived there himself.

It's like that, Arkie considered, watching him as he sat eating next to Jo, mum and Michael. *It's like he lives here. Once, just once, I wish his mum would come up here and tell him to come home. Except she never will.*

"We need a new toaster, Mike," mum announced as she stood over at the cupboards next to the sink. "It's making charcoal instead of toast."

Michael rolled his eyes. "Bloody thing. They don't make toasters like they used to." He engrossed himself in the newspaper.

"What're we doing today?" Jo asked in a desperate voice. "Anything?"

"Are we going out anywhere?" Arkie added.

Mum sat herself down, and buttered two slightly burnt pieces of toast. "Michael and I were thinking of checking the markets out this afternoon — "

"Aw great!"

"— seeing as how we haven't been for months," mum finished.

"Good, I need some new clothes," Arkie said.

"Don't we all?" mum remarked.

"Can Ian come too?" Jo asked.

"If it's all right by his mum," Michael answered.

'Course it'll be all right. "Can I buy something at the markets, mum?"

Mum nodded.

"Great, thanks," Arkie replied.

"A pleasure. Remember me when I'm old and grey."

"Sure, mum."

As breakfast wound down and concluded, both boys edged themselves close to Michael.

"What happened to your face?" Jo asked, tracing a finger over the faded, pocked skin beneath Michael's cheekbone.

"I had acne."

"What's that?"

"Teenage disease. Pimples."

"Oh. And you've got a mark here, under your lip."

"I was hit by someone."

"Who?" Jo persisted.

"Just someone," Michael answered patiently, setting his newspaper down on the table and looking at Jo and Ian in turn.

"When you were a kid or a grown-up?" Jo asked.

"When I was a kid."

Jo looked puzzled and thoughtful.

Then Ian said, "You haven't got as much hair as you used to have," and brushed a timid hand across Michael's slightly receded hairline.

Arkie looked up from her perusal of the other newspapers' Sunday comics, in time to see Michael smile slightly and say, "Don't remind me, mate."

The first kid I ever met from school here was Ian, because he came up that morning to stickybeak at the removal van when it unloaded all our stuff. It was the day we moved here and Ian kept wiping his runny nose on his sleeve and saying to us, "Who are you? What are you doing here at Michael's house?"

"Let's go and kick the soccer ball around," Jo said to Ian, and the pair of them filed out the back door. Michael followed them outside as well, with the intention of doing some gardening.

Arkie sprawled herself across the patch of sunlight that spilled through one loungeroom window, and flicked through the Sunday papers in search of interesting reading. Mum came in from cleaning up the kitchen and settled herself at the piano. Flipping the lid gently up, she played scales for a moment or so, her fingers gliding backwards and forwards over the keys. Then she sat, for ages it seemed, in a gazing silence.

Arkie looked up to see her mum reach for the power switch on the reel-to-reel tape, and the reels started rewinding with their characteristic high-pitched whirr. The stop and play buttons were pressed in turn then, and music sailed forth from the loudspeaker on the floor.

Whenever mum did play her tapes back — and there were a dozen or more boxes of them lined up on top of the piano — it was surprising to hear the other things beside music that had found their way into the microphones: Michael, Arkie, Jo and sometimes Ian talking and calling out, Headley in the yard barking, kids from down the street whooping around in the backyard, and once in a while, mum's own murmuring voice as she talked about the music she was recording. "All sorts of ambient sounds," she told Arkie, because the music was sometimes also accompanied by wind and the tinkling windchimes, birds in the trees outside, the electric kettle whistling and switching itself off, rain clattering against the windows.

"Those tapes are like a photo album of this house," Michael said once, "without the photos. They're a permanent account of living here at the top of Ramsay Street."

The tape played on, symphonic and flowing. With a pencil, mum followed the melody across a handwritten musical score sheet. The music finished, and she clicked the tape deck off, before switching the synthesizer on and programming a drum and percussion beat.

"I like this dance stuff you play," Arkie said over the rattle and thump coming out of the loudspeaker. "Sort of outer space dance music."

"Thanks," mum said, glancing back at her.

"You ought to join a band or something," Arkie added, thinking of the polaroid photos in one of her mum's albums; pictures of mum with four or five friends from teachers' college, who were all brandishing instruments. "Like that band you used to be in.'

"Huh," mum replied, "we played together for about six months, argued with each other the whole time, and played nothing but songs by other people. We never got around to writing our own songs."

"When I was eight, I told the kids at school that you used to play in a rock band."

"And?"

"And they didn't believe me until I showed them the photos. Jay Riley —"

"Who?"

"Jay Riley — in our class at school — his dad plays guitar in some band..."

Mum sighed. The synthesiser was still playing a repetitive percussion beat. "Sometimes I get sick of making tapes and filing them away like finished schoolwork. I *would* like to join a band again, actually." She shook her head, as if clearing these thoughts from her mind, and began picking a hesitant melody out on the piano.

Arkie stood up and made a brief trip to her bedroom. "Can I take a photo?" she asked, returning with the camera.

"Every time I look at you these days, you've got that camera in your hand," mum said, persisting with the melody. "What d'you want me to do? Smile? Look serious?"

"Just keep on playing..." Arkie replied softly, peering through the camera's viewfinder at the slightly hazy image of her mum bent over the piano's keyboard. *Click*. "Okay mum, relax. Got you."

"Thanks," her mum said with a slight grin. "I want t' see all these photos when you finally get them printed —"

"Yeah."

"— and now," she went on with resolve, adjusting one of the microphone stands and arching the mike close to the piano keys, "I'm going to tape something."

When Arkie returned to her room, she was startled by the sight of Michael, in the garden immediately outside the window. "What're you doing?" she called to him through the glass.

He held up a pair of secateurs and called back, "Giving this bush a slight pruning. Giving you a bit of sunlight and a view."

"Not too much," she said loudly, remembering too late that her mum probably had the tape recorder going in the loungeroom. "I don't want everybody stickybeaking in through the window at me."

He gestured back as if to say "No worries," and began to snip at the shrub that until now had all but obliterated any view there was. And gradually, the window admitted shafts of morning light and a leafy, fragmented scene of the garden, Ramsay Street and the shimmering ocean. Michael left it at that, and walked away to garden somewhere else.

Mum's music was making the floorboards vibrate.

Arkie looked over at the roll-top desk. *I'll clean the rest of it out soon, Michael said.* She slid the desk drawers open and shut until she came to one of the collections of photo envelopes. Clasping one, she went over to the couch beneath the window. The music in the loungeroom diminished and ended, sending the house into near silence. From outside came vague noises — traffic, bits of Jo's conversation with Ian, a sharp click or two as Michael pruned elsewhere in the garden. Numb with some sort of anticipation, Arkie opened the envelope and pulled out a dozen or so school photographs of various sizes. She knew — even before spotting *Michael Byrne* in typewritten letters, along with all the other children's names — whose photos they would all be, and searched each photo in turn for Michael's face. There was one of him as a tiny kindergarten child, others of him in primary school and finally high school, his face narrowing with age. The rows of children in school uniforms aged and changed with him, smiling, grinning and smirking as much as the respective teachers and photographers had allowed. But Michael, without exception, carried the expression that Arkie had first seen in the music-camp photograph, distant and unsmiling, as if gazing at a vision of his own making.

Why isn't he smiling? It troubled Arkie somewhat. She flicked through the photographs once more, and the sunlight filtering through the window caught long-ago children's faces in flashes of glare. *It's like a jigsaw puzzle with pieces missing.* She looked over at the desk drawers, certain that more puzzle pieces were to be found within. *Don't clean the desk out too soon, Michael.*

From the loungeroom, her mum called, "Arkie, did you want to ask Kylie along to the markets with us this afternoon?"

"Kylie's going out," Arkie replied, and felt certain that mum knew it wasn't the truth.

At school, Kylie directed her talk and attentions elsewhere. She wrote secret notes in class and had them furtively passed along to Rebecca so that the two of them could exchange knowing glances and sign language when Mr Clifton wasn't looking. The notes, glances and gestures were not explained to Arkie, and she felt increasingly irritated by it all. The desk she and Kylie shared seemed to become possessed of an invisible boundary line after Kylie asked Mr Clifton one day if the class could change their seating arrangements.

"You've already changed around once this term," he replied. "Wait until after the holidays."

"But I've been in the same seat all year," Kylie protested, glancing quickly in Arkie's direction, and frowning and pouting for Mr Clifton's benefit.

"After the holidays," Mr Clifton repeated.

"Thanks a lot," Arkie muttered to Kylie, who was busy exchanging irritated looks with Rebecca.

Arkie queued in the noisy canteen lines at lunch break, and then escaped into the bustle of the playground. She walked past games of hop-scotch and elastics, a group of kids playing chasings between the toilets and bubblers, teachers on playground duty clenching mugs of tea and edging their way between jostling children. There was a large texta-drawn poster of a bunyip on the glass door of the school library, and carnival lettering that announced *We're open, come in!* Beyond the cluster of post-war brick classrooms was the expanse of grass playground, at the rear of the school and safely away from the main road. Here, she found Mr. Clifton.

"Welcome to playground duty," he remarked to her. "Joy of my life, it is. Retrieving footballs from trees, chasing kids from out of bounds areas,

breaking up fights, sending bleeding knees and
noses off for treatment. Wonderful stuff." He had
a mandatory cup of tea in one hand; his other hand
being grasped firmly by a small kindergarten boy.
"So where's the rest of our class today?" Mr
Clifton asked. "You're all usually hanging around
together somewhere."

Arkie shrugged. "I dunno. Playing chasings or
something."

"Sounds exciting," he said dryly.

"It's not," Arkie answered emphatically.

Mr Clifton turned to the kindergarten boy.
"Hey Vic, how would you like to do a really
important job for me? Yes? Here's some money.
Can you go and line up in the canteen and buy
me a chocolate Paddle Pop? It has to be chocolate,
not something urky like banana or bubblegum.
Okay?" He handed over a dollar coin, and the boy
ran off, zigzagging enthusiastically between ball
games and groups of kids.

Mr Clifton had a sip of tea. "I missed my
calling, I should have gone into slave trading."

Arkie grinned. That was what she liked about
Mr Clifton, he was a human being and he had a
sense of humour. He was interesting to look at too,
because his appearance altered with every twist of
magazine fashion. His hair was prickly and had a
subtle streak of colour through it, he wore pointy
boots, a shirt that looked like a tablecloth and a
baggy pair of trousers that looked like something
out of a black and white movie. "What was it like
when you were at school?" she asked.

Mr Clifton looked surprised. "When I was at

school?" he replied. His voice was husky, as though he had a permanent cold. "Well...it was a Catholic school in a sleepy country town. It was one and a half hours by bus each day, and sometimes I'd fall asleep on the way home. And my favourite teacher was Sister Michelle, who was really old and wore a black habit. She was more like everybody's grandma than everyone's teacher —"

"Is that why you became a teacher?"

"I dunno, possibly. I didn't want t' be a farmer and I wanted to live in the city. Teaching happened accidentally, I guess."

"Is this the first school you've been at?"

He shook his head and started walking. "I taught around the inner city for a while. It was okay. Smoggy and noisy, but okay. Your mum's a teacher, isn't she?"

"Yeah, she's a music teacher at the high school. But she plays music all the time. She's always writing music and taping music —"

"What instrument?"

"A piano. She's got a synthesizer as well."

"Great!" Mr Clifton was quietly impressed. "The only noise in my house when I was a kid was the television; rural news and American soap operas. My dad would be out on a tractor until dark each day, then he'd come in and sit in front of the television in a trance. He still does."

"I'd like to see a photo of you when you were little."

Mr Clifton laughed. "Arkie, you wouldn't recognise me. I used to look very sweet and innocent. My parents are horrified about the way I look these days." He paused and looked sideways at her. "Why all this interest about me so suddenly?"

"I just wondered."

"Not that I mind. You're the first person who's ever asked at this school."

Vaguely embarrassed, Arkie fell silent. They had walked up to the windows of their own classroom, and Mr Clifton pushed one window open. "How's it going in there, mate?" he asked, because Ian Koh was walking around the classroom setting up the desks for an afternoon of art.

"Okay," Ian replied quietly, setting down paintbrushes next to palettes of paint.

"Sure you don't want a hand? Arkie can come in and help, if you like."

Ian shook his head. "I can manage alright. Everything's nearly done, anyway."

Mr Clifton nodded. "Thanks for your help, Ian," he said, and turned to walk off. Arkie looked through the window into the classroom a moment longer, in time to see Ian smile to himself and continue handing out paintbrushes. *He likes Mr Clifton the way he likes Michael. Some mornings before school, he sits out near the carpark and waits for Mr Clifton to drive in.*

Mr Clifton was looking at his watch and mumbling, "Roll on, bell time," but then Vic the kindergarten boy returned and handed Mr Clifton a chocolate Paddle Pop and a handful of sticky change. "Ah, lunch at last!" he remarked, pulling a face so that Vic grinned before clasping the teacher's free hand once more.

Kylie, Rebecca and four or five other girls sauntered across in a laughing, conspiring huddle. "Hey, Mr Clifton, we've come to annoy you," Rebecca announced.

"Oh goody," Mr Clifton replied in a flat voice.

"Adam Black's looking for you," Kylie said to Arkie.

"Shut up," Arkie replied in annoyance. "He is not."

Kylie nodded, daring Arkie to react any further in front of Mr Clifton, "Adam's looking for you —"

"Mr Clifton," one of the other girls began, "Rebecca wants to know —"

"I do not!"

"Rebecca wants to know if you've got a girlfriend!"

"Mr Clifton, I didn't say that —"

"Mr Clifton, Rebecca's dad said he saw you in the pub down at Manly with a good-looking girl."

"Wooo, Mr Clifton, who was she?"

"We didn't think teachers went to pubs, Mr Clifton."

"Who was the girl, Mr Clifton?"

Mr Clifton took a patient bite of his Paddle Pop and regarded the group with surprising tolerance. "I'm not saying anything."

The girls broke into a chorus of: "Awww sssir!"

Tell them to go jump.

"What else have your parents been saying?" Mr Clifton asked them. "Come on, my turn to ask the questions. What else have they been saying?"

Kylie, Rebecca and the others exchanged glances. "My mum reckons you look more like a pop star instead of a teacher," Kylie volunteered.

Mr Clifton just about gagged on his Paddle Pop. "I can't even sing in time to the songs on the school radio programmes; you know that. What else?"

"What about all the kindergarten mums, waiting after school to pick up their little darlings every day —"

"The way they seem to wait at the seats outside *our* classroom —"

"— and stickybeak through the window at *you*, Mr Clifton —"

"How does it feel to be a heart throb, Mr Clifton?"

How does it feel to be an idiot, Kylie?

Mr Clifton shook his head and looked bemused. "I've never really thought about it —" he started to answer, but was interrupted by the shrill of the end-of-lunch bell.

The girls wandered away, calling back, "We'll see you when you're on playground duty next time, Mr Clifton."

"Great," Mr Clifton mumbled, and looked down at Vic. "Time to go and line up, mate."

"Are you on playground duty tomorrow?" Vic asked in a squeaky voice.

"Not until next Monday," Mr Clifton answered in a tone of great rejoicing. "Can you last until then, mate?"

Vic's shirt buttons were matched up to the wrong buttonholes, and part of his lunch was still decorating his chin. "Yeah," he answered with a sudden smile, and ran off to be lost amongst the kids stampeding for the toilets and bubblers.

"And what d' you think about Kylie wanting to change seats?" Mr Clifton asked in a serious voice.

The question had come out of the blue, and Arkie paused. Then she said, "Kylie can do whatever she likes; I don't care."

Mr Clifton nodded. "Mm, I understand." He looked around the playground, as the last of the kids sprinted across from far boundaries towards the classrooms. "I bet Ian's still inside setting up the art stuff," Mr Clifton added quietly.

"He prob'ly is," Arkie said.

Mr Clifton sighed. "I worry about that boy sometimes," he said, walking off toward the centre playground where the kids were lining up and teachers were already shouting commands.

SIX

"Is that your teacher?" Arkie's grandmother asked, peering through her ornate reading glasses at the class photo brought home from school that day.

Sometimes she really reminds me of mum. Sometimes I think they look exactly the same, but when nan speaks she says everything so differently.

"That's Mr Clifton," Arkie replied.

Nan shook her head, her lively blue eyes darting in Arkie's direction and then back at the photo in a gaze of final judgement. "Goodness, they're letting all sorts in these days."

"He's a good teacher," Arkie went on, "he's the most interesting teacher I've ever had —"

"I don't doubt that for a second."

"I mean, he teaches interesting things. Even the boring stuff he makes interesting for us —"

"And why aren't you smiling?" nan enquired. "Don't you smile for photographs any more?"

"I look like a vampire when I smile."

Nan rolled her eyes. "Nonsense. I think I prefer you smiling in photographs."

"Well, I was smiling a bit."

The radio station on the stereo had been changed, and orchestras and willowy love songs lent a different backdrop to the loungeroom. Nan had also sent Ian home and dispatched a disgruntled Jo to the bathroom upstairs. It was like this whenever nan came to look after them, the house becoming quieter, restrained and bound by unshakeable order. The downstairs rooms would become laced with the soft hint of the Cussons soap and floral fragrance nan used, the rattle of her jewellery and the click of her leather high heels on the floorboards.

"Go and put slippers on, please," she said to Jo when he came downstairs, his hair wet and his body caked in talcum powder. "It's the wrong time of year for bare feet."

"Elbows off the table, please," she reminded Arkie as they ate dinner.

From the loungeroom windows nan's silver BMW sedan could be seen, parked incongruously behind Michael's grotty utility. Michael and mum had taken themselves out for a meal together, as they sometimes did. *And afterwards, probably to a pub to see a band play, knowing mum.*

When nan takes Jo and I out in the BMW, she drives slowly all the way to the city and always seems to know when Jo's pulling faces at other drivers. We go into the big David Jones store and she buys us going out clothes and we have lunch in one of those little arcade cafes.

"Bedtime for you, I think," nan said to Jo. "School tomorrow."

Jo pulled a face. "Can you read to me, please?

Michael's been reading me this funny book by Roald Dahl called —"

"Clean those teeth first," nan ordered. "I'll be upstairs shortly. Arkravi, you and I might get this washing up out of the way." She always said Arkie's entire name, never the abbreviation. Jo was poking his tongue out triumphantly at Arkie and making rude hand signals as he climbed the stairs. Nan was already clattering dishes in the kitchen.

When nan went upstairs and began reading to Jo in her clipped, clear voice, Arkie took herself past the flickering television and sat down at the piano. The couch-side light and the TV were all that illuminated the loungeroom, and Arkie gazed in silence at the switches, dials and settings on the reel-to-reel and sythesizer. *Nan doesn't like the music mum plays much.* Once, mum had given Arkie's grandmother a cassette tape of gentle, flowing music, and nan had afterwards said plainly, "It didn't sound like anything much to me, Susan. What about the classical pieces you learnt as a child?"

The piano lid was open and a music score book sat perched upon it. Musical notes and worded phrases were dotted and marked over the pages in her mum's felt-pen handwriting.

Mum asked me when I was seven if I wanted to learn the piano, and because Kylie wasn't learning a musical instrument, I said no. Maybe I should've said yes.

Arkie stared down at the array of black and white keys that her mother had mastered so well.

Absently, she pressed a white key down, and the note echoed through the house like a doorbell.

"And what have you been doing lately, Arkravi?" nan asked later, when the two of them were sitting on the loungeroom couch with at least part of their attention focused on the television.

Arkie shrugged. "Homework. Reading books. And Michael gave me a camera, and I've been taking photos. It's a good camera, really old. Even Michael's not sure how old it is."

"What else?"

"Nothing really."

"Nothing? Heavens, when I was your age, I was on the go the whole time. Riding lessons, girl guides..."

But I'm not you, am I? I'm me, Arkie, and I've spent every lunchtime this week by myself, apart from talking in the playground once with Mr Clifton.

"What about your dancing lessons?"

"That was last year, nan, and I've stopped going."

"Why?"

"I just got tired of it. I wanted to do something different."

Nan sighed. An evening current affairs programme was on TV, and momentarily she involved herself with it.

"I've got my own room now, nan."

"I know, dear. I heard all about it from your mother and I had a quick look when I arrived this evening."

95

"D' you like it?"

"Very nice, apart from that cupboard full of . . . things."

"That's the Atrocity Cabinet, nan. All my treasures."

"Heavens above."

Their conversation subsided and the television's voice and music took over, as a documentary explained and depicted. On the floor and aimed at nan's feet, the portable fan heater hummed softly. As the documentary finally concluded and another programme began, nan said, "Bedtime for you, Arkravi."

"Can I read for a while?"

"Ten minutes only. Oh, and I believe Jo has to be woken up about now, to avoid," she finished heavily, "*accidents.* I thought he'd grown out of that."

"He's getting better," Arkie replied. "He's only wet once this week. Michael's had a star chart going, and that's —"

"Jo's too old to be wetting the bed. I suppose I'd better go and wake him."

"It's alright, I'll do it." When nan looked doubtful, Arkie added, "It's okay, I've done it before."

When she climbed the stairs and entered the bedroom, she paused for a moment, and stared into the semi-darkness at where her bed used to be. In its place was an expanse of floor, where Jo and Ian had built a space station out of Lego. *I used to really like this room.* She felt an odd twinge of regret.

In his bed, Jo was breathing a deep sleep. With a compassionate smirk, Arkie nudged him awake, gently eased him out of bed and walked him towards the hallway.

"What do . . . ?" he mumbled incoherently, his feet shuffling unevenly on the floor.

"It'd take a nuclear blast to wake you up," Arkie whispered, pushing the bathroom door open and turning on the light. When she had walked him over to the toilet, he seemed to have woken enough to realise what he was there for, and she watched indifferently as he spouted pee.

"No flood for you tonight," she said quietly, walking him back into the bedroom and helping him into bed.

From the street she caught the sound of voices, and walked over to the window. From here could be seen the familiar sweep of Ramsay Street by night, but the voices were close by. A little way beyond where the new units were being built, Sean Taylor's parents stood on the footpath outside the units where they lived. Mrs Taylor was next to her car and in going out clothes, Mr Taylor was in a T-shirt and jeans, and he was shouting.

Cautiously, Arkie unlatched one window and swung it quietly open. The voices echoed back, angrily and distinct. " . . . And where were you, then?" she heard Mr Taylor shout.

"On the way home from work, of course!" Mrs Taylor shouted back.

Arkie crouched down for a more unobtrusive view. She could see them clearly, illuminated as they were by street light, and felt guiltily sure that

97

if they had looked sideways up the hill, they would have seen her face staring back at them.

They continued shouting, and then Mr Taylor hit Mrs Taylor. She reeled back against the car, but just as quickly launched herself back at her husband and cuffed him across the face. "I've just as much right as you to go somewhere after work for a couple of quiet drinks with friends!" she yelled.

Further down the street, a couple of other people had walked out onto their balconies to see what was happening. Mr Taylor stalked off inside then, and Arkie was just about to close the window when, with sudden horror, she saw him return with a hammer in his hand. He brushed past his wife and with a resounding crash, sent the hammer through the windscreen of her car. More neighbours had wandered outside to investigate by now, and a group of them had assembled on the footpath opposite. Mr Taylor heaved the hammer through the car's back window then, and started on the side windows. There was glass sprayed over the car's bonnet. Mrs Taylor was in tears and shouting angrily. With renewed alarm, Arkie caught sight of the Taylor children standing in the front yard of their units. Sean was clutching the hands of his younger brother and sister, and shouting incoherently at his father.

Mr Taylor stormed inside.

I've heard them fight before, but never like that. I've never seen anyone fight like that before. Poor Sean.

Arkie eased the window closed and crept over

to the bathroom. Numbed, she brushed her teeth and stared, expressionless, at her reflection in the mirror. When she returned downstairs, nan was over at the loungeroom windows. "What was all that noise down the street?" she asked Arkie in an anxious voice.

"Two people having a fight," Arkie replied flatly. "Car windows were getting broken."

"How do you know?"

"I saw it all from the bedroom window. They were the parents of one of the kids in my class."

Nan was shaking her head. To herself, more than anyone else, she said, "It's these beachside suburbs and these home units —"

Next day at school, the street scene bounced around in Arkie's mind on continual replay. The lines at morning assembly buzzed with hushed conversations behind cupped hands.

"Did you hear what happened in our street last night?"

"I heard it."

"I saw it."

"Her car windows got smashed —"

"Sean's dad did it with a hammer —"

"My mum was gonna call the cops."

"Sssh."

Sean Taylor kept a grim, detached silence.

The lines of kids shuffled and fidgeted restlessly as teachers took the loudspeaker in turn to make announcements or reprimands.

"These lines are a disgrace!" Mrs King's voice crackled over the loudhailer. She was the deputy principal and in her usual cranky, military mood. "Look at that class over there! I can't even see a boys' line and a girls' line! Is that sixth class, is it?"

"We have two lines over here. My class has two lines of children," Mr Clifton called back valiantly. Most of the school and all of the teachers were looking at him. "Boys and girls can stand in either line if they're in my class."

Mrs King looked dubiously at him, grunted and directed a reprimand at another class.

"Wow, who'd have her for a teacher?" Kylie whispered.

"D'you reckon she knows how to smile?" Arkie whispered, and felt gratified when Kylie grinned and shook her head in reply.

At last, the announcements came to a close, and the mass of children dispersed to their various classrooms. For Arkie's class at least, here was where the boredom finished, because Mr Clifton had injected his own classroom with enthusiasm and a surprising contentment. The walls inside were always lined with illustrated projects the kids had worked on; artwork hung from bulletin boards and the ceiling, mice scrambled around a cage near the cushioned book corner and fish swam lazily around a cupboard-top tank, inviting contemplation by anyone who needed a moment's break from algorisms or spelling lists. Children from other classes peered through the windows at playtime, envying the occupants of Mr Clifton's room. The corner of the ceiling where the rain leaked through and the noise from the nearby main road were drawbacks Arkie's class were willing always to overlook.

Sometimes, I'm lucky.

"End-of-week evaluation today," Mr Clifton said brightly. "A maths test here, a spelling test there."

Inevitably, a few kids groaned.

"Why, sir?"

"Yeah, why?"

"Because that's life. And because Mrs King says so. But look on the bright side, it's Friday."

A few polite cheers greeted this.

"Right," Mr Clifton went on, "who's talking to us this morning?" He had two gold sleepers in one ear and was flicking them with his index finger.

Eric Lomas and Sally Devries stood up and walked to the front of the room, Eric bearing a couple of newspaper clippings and Sally with a book brought from home.

"Okay," Mr Clifton began, ready to hear the dissertation each child was to deliver. But then he slapped his hand to his forehead. "No, stop, stop. Sorry." He rummaged around on his desk. "Lucky, lucky me has been put in charge of the sports carnival this year — no, stop laughing, Kylie Bethel, I can play *some* sport — and I need team numbers sorted out for the school and various jobs sorted out for the teachers." He pulled out a clipboard with stencilled paper attached. "Sorry, Eric and Sally, you can relax for a couple of minutes. I need a messenger —"

"Aw sir!"

"Sir!"

"Me, sir!"

"— to hustle around the entire school, asking teachers to fill these sheets out. I need it done by morning break...no, Warren Goldburg, you've gone on more messages this week than I've got hands and feet."

"Aw sir!"

"And will you stop calling me sir? It makes me feel old and grey."

Hands were waving in the air, keen for the message-running. Sean Taylor didn't have his hand up, and he was staring at his desk.

"Same with you, Brett Falwell," Mr Clifton said, "you've been out of the room so much this week, I almost forget what you look like. Arkie, you'll do."

Whilst others grumped and pulled faces, Arkie bounced out of her seat, feeling very pleased. With the clipboard, a pen and a quick brief from Mr Clifton she left the classroom, smiling triumphantly at the other kids and giving a royalty-style wave before escaping into the sunlight outdoors.

"Do hurry back," Mr Clifton had intoned as she'd shut the door behind her. "We'll miss you terribly." And the class laughed.

Arkie drifted from classroom to classroom with the clipboard and pen, enjoying the brief change from school routine. The noise of other classes settling into morning work greeted her at each door, and the voices of teachers, ranging from friendly to resigned. Other classrooms were interesting to look at anyway, especially the ones Arkie had resided in during previous school years.

Soon enough, she reached Jo's room.

"Come in," said a weary voice, above a continuing babble of voices.

Miss Sereni was marking the roll and her class sat on the carpet in front of her. Some were squirming or fidgeting, and one kid was moving surreptitiously towards concealment behind a group of desks every time Miss Sereni ducked her head to read a name from her class list.

A couple of kids, Jo included, were doing a good job of pretending to be angels, sitting up with false straightness and adopting looks of phony sincerity.

Huh, Arkie thought, figuring where and how Jo received the red smiley and star stamps that were often tattooed in stamp-pad ink on his forehead or hand when he came home some afternoons.

"Yes," inquired the teacher in a slightly edgy tone, "what?"

"Some things to fill in for the sports carnival, miss," Arkie replied, "from Mr Clifton."

Jo was making his eyebrows jump up and down for Arkie's benefit.

Miss Sereni sighed. "Look, would you mind waiting a couple of minutes? I want to get this roll marking finished. RIGHT," she said to the class, and they momentarily froze. "Mark Chappell?"

"Here, miss."

"Darryl Eady?"

"Here, miss."

"Martha Lewis, for the last time, would you leave Kate's hair alone? This is not a beauty salon." Miss Sereni huffed to herself and resumed marking the roll. A few kids were looking at each other and giggling.

I'm glad I'm not a grotty little seven-or eight-year-old any more. And who'd want to be a teacher?

"Jo Gerhardt?"

"Here, miss." Jo was seated right in front of her, where she could not fail to notice his attempts at appearing faultless for the subdued mayhem happening around him.

Arkie glared at him, and mouthed "Don't be such a crawler", for him to lipread.

There was a knock at the door and a small girl wandered in with a vague look on her face and wet, combed-down hair.

"Kelly Thompson, why are you late? Again?" Miss Sereni asked.

"Miss, mum said to tell you she slept in and couldn't get us our breakfasts in time."

"Oh, sit down. Buy your mum a new alarm clock for her birthday."

"Pardon, miss?"

"Nothing. Mark Jackson?"

A squeal. "Here, miss."

"Mark and Justine, what are you doing?"

"Mark's tickling me, miss."

"Mark —"

"Miss, she's following me all over the mat. Whenever I move, so does—"

"BOTH OF YOU — stop your fooling. Move away from each other."

There was another knock at the door. Miss Sereni rolled her eyes and glared past Arkie, who by now was leaning against the *How tall are we?* chart. "Come in!" she called.

Another primary school kid, a boy, walked in clutching an armful of class roll books. "Rolls, miss!" he said brightly, but was instantly withered by Miss Sereni's glare.

"Would you mind waiting. . . there at the end of the queue. I'll be finished in a moment."

Once, Jo told me that he walked into his classroom at lunchtime to get something and found Miss Sereni at her desk, crying over a pile of flashcards.

When finally Arkie returned with the clipboard and stencilled sheets, the climate in her own classroom had altered slightly.

Mr Clifton was rather edgily going through the previous night's homework, and someone at the back of the room was making bird noises. Mr Clifton couldn't work out who was responsible. "Look," he said, "I'd appreciate that person making those noises to cut it out, unless they'd prefer doing a bit of detention at lunchtime."

Arkie resumed her seat next to Kylie and picked up the threads of the homework being corrected. She went through her completed maths stencil as Mr Clifton dictated or requested answers. The bird noises continued.

"LOOK," Mr Clifton interrupted himself loudly, "whoever you are, you're going to ruin my Friday and everyone else's if I wind up cranky. Cut the noises out."

The homework correcting resumed, and so

did the noises at odd intervals, except that now they were less like bird noises and more like fart noises.

"Last warning," Mr Clifton said with forced calm.

Another noise,

This time, Mr Clifton spotted the culprit. "Sean, get yourself out here, please."

Sean Taylor shuffled out, not smiling.

"What do you think you're up to?" Mr Clifton said, leaning over slightly so that he was at eye level with Sean. "What's with all the nonsense?"

Sean didn't answer.

"I've asked you a question, Sean, would you mind answering?"

Sean shook his head slowly, as tears welled up in his eyes and ran down his cheeks. He brushed them away fiercely with one hand and remained silent.

The other kids exchanged knowing looks. Concern crossed Mr Clifton's face, and he said quietly, "Take yourself outside. Wash your face and have a drink of water. I'll be out shortly."

Sean shuffled out of the room, obscuring his face from the class's collective gaze.

Mr Clifton raised his eyebrows, looked thoughtful and asked, "Does anyone know what's happened?"

The class exchanged more looks amongst themselves, and most shook their heads in reply.

"Did anything happen in the playground before school?" Mr Clifton pressed. "Or on the way to school? Someone must know."

Shrugs and more head shakes.

Then Adam Black put up his hand and said sombrely, "Sean's parents had a big fight last night. Some of us saw it." He fell silent then and looked about quickly and anxiously, as if doubting the wisdom of having said anything.

Mr Clifton heaved an audible sigh and muttered a soft curse. "I'm glad you told me," he said quietly.

SEVEN

Broken glass, still littered the gutter in Ramsay
Street a week after the fight. The Taylors' car was
parked in more or less its usual position next to
the kerb, the windscreen and back window having
been replaced. Two side windows remained
screened with clear plastic fastened by strips of
sticky tape. Arkie passed the debris every day on
the way to school. The sight of it made her feel
strange and vaguely alarmed, as did the time when
she met Mrs Taylor in the newsagency and they'd
exchanged the usual hellos, as if nothing had
happened.

That same afternoon, Arkie had wandered into
the local bank to leave some pocket money in her
account, and Ian's mother was there, standing at a
teller's window. She was smartly, almost elabor-
ately, dressed, yet her slightly dishevelled hair and
lined, anxious face rendered her outfit awkward.
Ian stood close beside her. He was talking to her
softly and when he spotted Arkie in an adjacent
line of waiting customers, he waved but did not
smile.

Now it seemed strange, too, to be walking to where Kylie lived, after weeks of not having done so.

"Oh," Kylie said after answering Arkie's door-knock. "Hi. Come in."

"Who is it?" called Kylie's mum from the loungeroom.

"Arkie," Kylie called back, ushering Arkie into her bedroom. "How come you're here?" she asked flopping down onto her bed. "You haven't visited for ages."

"Just thought I'd see what you were up to," Arkie answered, because she had expected Kylie to be occupied with Rebecca's company.

"Oh."

One wall of Kylie's bedroom was plastered with pop star pictures. Dolls in different national costumes were ranged along a windowsill, and a small collection of cosmetics littered the top of a mirrored dressing table.

Arkie knelt down on the carpeted floor and said, "Michael wanted to know if you were going away anywhere these school holidays and whether or not you could look after Headley and Goodvibes for us, because we're going away."

Kylie shrugged. "Mum has to work, doesn't she, so I'm not going anywhere to stay. Where are you going?"

"Up north. One of mum's friends lives in a farmhouse out the back of somewhere."

"Sounds exciting," Kylie said sarcastically. "Yeah, I guess I can. What's Michael gonna pay me this year?"

"Thirty dollars for the fortnight, provided you can take Headley for a walk every day —"

"Yeah, sure, sure." Kylie's voice sounded wearily impatient, and she reached over to where a portable cassette deck sat next to her bed, pressing the play button so that shrill top ten music filled the bedroom.

It's different. It's not the same any more.

"I've been practising a dance routine," Kylie said loudly, over the noise of the music. She sprang up and pushed the bedroom door shut. "I saw the film clip for this song on TV last weekend and I think I've got the dance steps the way they had them on telly. Anyway, I've been practising —"

"What for?" Arkie asked.

"School disco, silly. It's next Friday. Aren't you going?"

"Yeah, I'm going —"

"I've almost got these steps right. Watch —" Kylie shimmied and strutted from one end of her bedroom to the other, her feet moving rhythmically over the carpet as the music played on. "Can't get those funny shoulder rolls, but. . .you have a go."

"Why?"

"Why? So that you can try this amazing dance routine out with Adam Black."

"Get out of it, Kylie."

"Alright, Robert Steeple, then."

"Steeple? Urk, are you kidding? He spends half the time posing off and the other half picking his nose."

"How d' you know?"

"Come on, watch him in class some time."

"Okay, how about Robert Checcutti?"

"Well at least he asks you to dance, and he doesn't flop around like a marshmallow —"

"Probably practises at home in front of the mirror —"

"Like several other people I could mention," Arkie added quickly.

Kylie smiled back at her strangely and said, "Well there's one person I'm not gonna dance with at any school disco and that's Koh."

"Ian? He's alright."

"Aw, he's a drip, Arkie. Last time we had a disco at school, he sat on a seat and just stared the whole night."

"Well, he's shy, he can't help that. He's always been —"

"And he's a crawler, too. Always hanging around Mr Clifton, always wanting to be super helpful."

"Ian's okay," Arkie said emphatically. "I feel sorry for him."

Kylie wrinkled her nose, shook her head and looked unimpressed. She reached over and stabbed at the cassette player buttons, rewinding the tape and then pressing the play button once more. "Come on," she said to Arkie with renewed energy that was as keen as it was bossy, "stand up and go through these dance steps with me."

Arkie stood up, feeling slightly less than enthusiastic. "How d' you start?" she asked.

"Like this, watch."

"Okay?"

"Right. Side step, side step, turn, shake. Keep going, roll your shoulders."

"How?"

"Watch me, twit! Just copy. Now faster. Knees, kick, turn —"

"Aargh!" Arkie gurgled, losing her balance, mostly on purpose, and collapsing in a heap on the quilt of Kylie's bed.

"Arkie, you're a show-off. Try it again."

This time they faced each other and repeated the dance steps across the room with a bit more success, except that Arkie battled the whole time to keep a straight face because Kylie seemed to be taking the whole thing so seriously.

"This is mad," Arkie remarked.

Kylie began to reply, but at that moment out in the hallway came a loud rapping at the front door. Kylie's mum walked past to open it and then said in a crisp, impatient voice, "Yes? What are you doing here today?"

"I've come to take Kylie out," came a man's voice.

Kylie's face dropped, and quietly she clicked her bedroom door open and peeked out quickly.

"Who is it?" Arkie asked in a low voice.

Kylie pushed the bedroom door quietly closed and in a panicky whisper answered, "My father, but he's not supposed to be here! It's once a month and he's already taken me out this month. What's he doing here?" She sank down onto the carpet and turned the music on the cassette player down slightly. She leant back against her bed and started to pick at her fingernails. "It's not this weekend," she whispered.

Out in the hallway, the voices escalated.

"Well you might've at least phoned —"

"I didn't have to! Last time I was here, we agreed —"

"We agreed nothing. One weekend a month is the standing arrangement."

"Aw come on —"

"It's been the arrangement for three or four years! What d' you take me for?"

"Last time, I asked about an extra Sunday this month! You shrugged your shoulders —"

"I did no such thing. We have a formal, legal agreement. Kylie has a friend around visiting and is otherwise occupied. Now, would you mind —"

"Don't shut the door in my face, thanks!"

"This is my house."

"Correction, flat. I'm the one with the house."

"Look, I didn't ask you around to brag. You didn't even phone in advance —"

"Kylie! Would you like to go out today?"

In the bedroom, Kylie sat on the carpet and said nothing. Arkie, not sure whether to sit down also or remain standing, walked awkwardly over to the window. *I don't want to be here. I don't want to hear any of this.*

"Kylie!" came her father's shout once more.

No answer.

"Would you mind just going?" came Kylie's mum's voice angrily. "In three more weeks, she will be available for an outing with you —"

The two voices faded slightly out onto the staircase landing. One set of footsteps clattered noisily down the stairs, another set walked back

113

into the flat. After the front door slammed came minutes and minutes of silence. In the bedroom, the cassette player continued its broadcast. Neither Arkie or Kylie said a word.

Then the bedroom door was pushed open, and Kylie's mum said quietly, "You okay?" She probably meant the query for both girls, but approached Kylie and knelt down next to her. "Hey Ky, are you alright?"

Kylie arched her face away from her mother and grumbled, "I'm alright." She went on picking at her fingers.

Kylie's mum grimaced and stood up. "I'm really sorry, Arkie. It wasn't a very nice thing to have had to listen to."

Arkie shrugged and forced herself to say, "It's okay. It doesn't matter."

Kylie punched the rewind button on her cassette player. Her mother regarded them both for a moment longer and then walked out. From the loungeroom came the rustle of a cigarette packet and the rasp of a lighter being used.

The cassette tape whirred, whined and then clicked to a stop. Kylie reached for the play button, and the dance music they had been shuffling to minutes before began again. Kylie would not look up, and levelled her gaze at her fingernails.

Arkie waited in vain for something to happen or something to be said.

"I have to go home," she told Kylie at last. "We're going out this arvo."

Kylie shrugged and mumbled, "Suits me."

Even before she reached the driveway at

114

home, Arkie could hear mum's and Michael's voices. The bonnet of the Batmobile was up, and Michael was occupied on the engine beneath, a screwdriver and spanner set scattered at his feet. Mum was weeding a nearby garden.

"Hullo," they chorused, and Michael added, "Back so soon?"

"Yeah."

"Did you ask Kylie about the pets?"

"I asked her and she said yes,"Arkie replied, walking through the carport and down the path towards the front door.

"Is anything wrong, Arkie?" mum called after her.

"No."

Jo was sprawled on one of the lounge chairs, a set of headphones clamped over his ears. He was singing loudly and discordantly to one of Michael's ancient Easybeats' records. Arkie sighed in mild exasperation and walked upstairs. Goodvibes was asleep on Jo's bed, and he blinked awake when Arkie walked in, regarding her with his usual blithely idiotic expression.

"Hello, dumb bum," she said softly, patting him roughly so that his ears flattened down. Goodvibes was a very tolerant cat.

She stared around the room at the expected clutter of Jo's possessions, as well as the last of her own things that hadn't yet been moved downstairs: a dilapidated collection of Enid Blyton books given over several Christmases by aunts, the carved wooden masks that had been mailed by nan from Fiji years before . . .

Our dad never came back at weekends. He's never invited Jo and me to stay with him in Perth during school holidays.

Outside, the Batmobile's bonnet was clunked shut, and Michael's footsteps scuffed down the path and indoors. She heard him say to Jo, "Hey tiger, you'll have to get yourself ready soon; we're visiting your nan, remember?" He sprinted up the stairs then and into the bathroom. Taps were squeaked on, water clattered into the bathtub and steam began to drift into the hallway. "Yuk! Glad I'm not a mechanic the rest of the week," came Michael's mumbled voice.

Arkie returned to her own room, closing the door behind her and going to the roll-top desk. She pulled another envelope of photos out and sat down on her bed.

Michael on his birthday bike, was written in neat, flowing pen on the back of one picture. *In the garden with dad*, was written on the back of another. Photo after photo showed Michael alone or with his parents, a boy between Jo's and Arkie's ages. In the background stood a plain brick cottage with a sparse, manicured garden; cars with interstate number plates.

She replayed the argument between Kylie's parents to herself, and explored her own memory for images of the flat she herself had once lived in. *I can't remember mum and dad shouting or fighting. I just remember when he left and didn't come back.*

Arkie's grandmother had photos, too. In the heavy

oak bookshelves that lined one wall of nan's ordered loungeroom was a whole row of albums. One album was nothing but pictures of mum's wedding. Stuck on the pages as well were newspaper announcements of the event, and a large picture from the social pages of a magazine — mum in a primrose-coloured wedding dress and Arkie's dad with a skinny bow tie and a tailed jacket. They were standing in a church doorway laughing, as a wind ruffled their hair.

Smiling down from the wall above the sideboard opposite were two framed photos, one of Arkie's mum and the other of nan's other daughter, Arkie's aunt. They both wore dark school uniforms and their hair was pulled back in plaits; each sat at a piano.

This must have been an amazing place to have grown up in. Arkie breathed in the odours of furniture polish and aerosol air freshener that seemed to permeate each grandly furnished room of the stately house.

"Why don't you boys go outside and hit a ball around the tennis court?" she heard nan saying to Jo and Ian in the next room. "The net's up and the racquets and balls are behind the door in the laundry."

"Where's Arkie?" mum asked. She, nan and Michael were seated around the dining table with cups of coffee and biscuits.

"She went outside, I think," Jo replied.

Arkie smiled to herself.

The boys' voices faded from earshot.

"That child," nan said, referring to Ian, "is

always with you. Does his mother ever look after him?"

"Not often," Michael said with a sigh. "She's got a bit of an alcohol problem. For a while she was okay, but it all seems to be getting worse again."

"It seems to me," nan continued, "that both of you are making a rod for your own backs, and that you're being used by his mother. Actually, it sounds like a matter for the child welfare people."

"They were involved once before," Michael said in a voice indicating he wanted to drop the subject, "but I've known Ian most of his life, and it's not an easy situation to make judgements about."

The conversation lapsed. There was the clink of cups on saucers. Arkie, out of view and listening intently, sat crosslegged on the carpet next to the bookshelves. Quietly, she pulled out another of the photo albums. This one began with photos of herself as a baby and toddler. In some of them she was being held by the grandfather who had died soon after her first birthday. There were the same sorts of baby and toddler photos of Jo then, and he and Arkie together: she in pigtails and school uniform, he with long hair and carnival-coloured preschool clothes.

"And how's school, Michael?" nan asked. She often spoke to Michael as though meeting him for the first time.

"Oh...okay. End of term coming up and all that. Susan and I have been busy with the half-yearly reports, lately..."

For a little while, the conversation centred around high school.

"I was talking with Arkravi the other week," nan said then. "She doesn't seem to have a lot in the way of interests."

"Oh..." Arkie heard her mum reply in measured disagreement, "I wouldn't say that. She's always up to something or other."

"No, I meant organised things. Like the dancing lessons she told me she'd given up on, or joining girl guides, perhaps."

"Guides doesn't appeal to Arkie, mum. I've asked her myself."

"Well, you enjoyed guides, Susan."

"Yes I did, mum, but Arkie is Arkie. She's old enough to make her own decisions. She's got a lot of homework from school this year, but she still finds time to read —"

"Just like you at that age," nan interrupted. "Always with your head in a book."

"Yes," said mum with a slight laugh.

"She's taken to photography in a big way," Michael said. "I'm pleased about that."

"Half the time when we look in her direction," mum added, "she's got her camera pointed at us!"

"That's as may be," nan continued, unconvinced, "but she doesn't appear — to me, anyway — to be sharing interests with other girls her age."

There was another pause. "She is going through a quiet time at the moment," mum conceded, "but that's what it's about when you're twelve years old sometimes; body changes, high school next year...Arkie's got plenty going for her, and Michael and I don't want to force her into anything she doesn't want to do or be part of."

Arkie slid the photo album away, slung her camera over one shoulder and stood up. *Thanks mum, I'm glad I heard that.* Quietly, she tiptoed out of the loungeroom, through the kitchen and laundry and into the backyard. The overcast sky emphasised the lush green of the neat lawn, bordered with gnarled liquidambers and shrubbery. There was a pergola in the centre of the yard, covered with sticks of winter-bare wisteria; wrought-iron garden furniture beneath. An old brick garage housed nan's BMW. There was no audible traffic noise at all, just the breeze and the occasional sound of voices in other people's backyards.

Arkie went down to the fenced tennis court at the rear of the yard, where Jo and Ian were hitting and missing a tennis ball.

"Hey you guys, come over here," she ordered, undoing the camera case.

The boys walked to the edge of the court. "Hey, she's gonna take a photo," Jo said.

"Jeez, you're brilliant," Arkie told him, clicking the settings around.

"I don't like photos," Ian said to nobody in particular.

"Hey," Jo responded, nudging Ian in the shoulder, "don't worry. It's a real camera, not a trick one. It doesn't squirt water or anything."

Ian rolled his eyes.

"Do something funny," Arkie instructed, so Jo

and Ian both held their tennis racquets like guitars and leant over, as though frantically playing them. She took that shot, and then two individual pictures, one of Jo who smiled and tried to go cross-eyed, the other of Ian, who tensed seriously and stood precisely and expressionlessly still.

"Hey mum," she asked in the car on the way home, "how come nan always calls me Arkravi and never Arkie?"

"Don't know," mum replied, busily navigating the Batmobile. "She doesn't like abbreviations, I guess."

"Well she always abbreviates Jo's name. Joachim. Jo."

Mum nodded. "Mm, she does. Bit of a mystery, isn't it?"

"At least she doesn't call me Ark, like some of the kids at school do —"

Beside her on the back seat, Jo and Ian exchanged smirks, and Jo whispered "Ark ark" to Ian, so that it sounded like a bird noise.

Arkie pulled a face and held a threatening fist in Jo's direction. "It's a real pain having an unusual name sometimes, y' know," she finished telling her mum.

"Well," mum replied, "Arkravi was a girl I met when I was overseas and visiting Greece. In fact, I stayed with her family for three months."

"I know, you've told me before. At least Jo's name sounds normal when you shorten it, but."

"After Jo was born," mum continued, "just

121

afterwards, your Auntie Beverly came to visit me in hospital and said in a whiny voice, 'Joachim? Isn't that a Jewish name?'"

"Well, is it?" Arkie inquired. She was speaking to her mother's reflection in the rear view mirror.

"I don't know and don't mind," mum replied. "It's biblical, that's all I know."

"It sounds German or something," Arkie said. "Like dad's name..."

"Hmm."

Michael lounged back on the front passenger seat, preoccupied and silent. *Michael on his birthday bike...In the garden with dad.*

"Michael —"

"Yes, Arkie?"

"What was the house like where you grew up?"

He turned around, puzzled as though he hadn't heard the question properly. "The house I grew up in?"

"Yeah."

He shrugged. "Brick and suburban," he answered obscurely, before adding, "It's not there any more."

"Why? How come?"

"It was pulled down for a shopping centre carpark."

"Whereabouts was it?"

"Caulfield. Close to Melbourne." He turned his head slightly, as if speaking more to mum than Arkie. "I went back there once, after they'd demolished a whole block of houses. It was weird walking on asphalt where my mum used to have her clothes hoist and her garden."

Arkie's mum nodded.

"Where are your parents now?" Arkie asked.

"Still in Caulfield," Michael replied. "Bought themselves a townhouse. I haven't seen it, but I believe it's quite nice . . ."

Why haven't we met your parents, Michael? Arkie meant to ask the question aloud, expect that Michael commented then, in a voice of great rejoicing, "Two more weeks of school, isn't that great?"

"You can't say that," said Ian.

"Why not?"

"You're a teacher. You're supposed to enjoy working."

"I enjoy my holidays, too," Michael retorted indignantly.

"We're going away," Jo said. "Up the country."

"I know," Ian replied.

"Do you think you'll be able to handle it, Jo?" Michael asked. "There's no pinball or space invader machines where we're going."

"Yes," Jo replied, clicking his tongue and wrinkling his nose.

"What're you going to do, Ian?" mum asked.

Ian took a breath and quickly glanced at everybody in the car. "My mum's giving me extra pocket money and I'm going into the city to see as many films as I want to. I'm going roller skating and to the zoo and I don't know what else, yet." He glanced around again, taking in everybody's nods and reactions, then sat back in his seat looking oddly satisfied.

Arkie caught a glimpse of her mother's slightly frowning expression in the rear view mirror. She cast a sidelong glance at Ian, who by now had settled his gaze on the passing view.

He's almost smiling, she thought, surprised at the unusual calm his face reflected.

EIGHT

"Aw how come, Mr Clifton?"

"Yeah, how come? Why are you leaving?"

"Your favourite class and all, Mr Clifton —"

Mr Clifton sat on the edge of his desk and, for several minutes, quietly listened to the disgruntled comments. Finally, he looked up at them and said slowly: "I've been teaching for six years now, and I decided the time had come for me to take a major break from it. Not just school holidays, but several months."

"Why now, but?" Sean Taylor called out. "What about waiting till the end of the year?"

"Because," Mr Clifton replied, "I'm intending coming back to work after Christmas. It won't be back to this school, so I want to start at my new school at the beginning of the new year. Think how it'd be for you all starting at a new school halfway through the year instead of at the beginning —"

"But why, Mr Clifton?"

Mr Clifton closed his eyes for a moment, sighed and answered, "Because I'm tired and need a change of scenery for a while. If you think it was an easy decision for me, you're wrong, because it

125

was hard. I've really enjoyed working with you, and I'm disappointed about not seeing you right through until the end of the year."

"Well, what happens to us then, sir?"

"Yeah, who's gonna be our teacher instead?"

Mr Clifton shrugged. "That I don't know. Whoever it is, I'm leaving my teaching programme and a whole bunch of lesson notes behind for them to read and follow —"

Rebecca said, "I hope we don't get Mrs Barlow."

"Mrs who?" Mr Clifton asked.

"Mrs Barlow," the class chorused, and Adam Black added, "She's a relief teacher that we've had before and she's awful."

"Yeah, urk."

"Hope she's not a friend of yours or anything, sir."

"We've had her a few times when you were off sick, Mr Clifton, and all she did all day was sit at your desk and knit —"

"And nag."

"And give us boring stencils she never even marked."

"Yeah, nag and knit, nag and knit."

"Ah yes," Mr Clifton said with a smile of recognition, "I've heard about Mrs Barlow before. I rather think you'll be having someone else."

"What are you going t' do for a whole term instead of teaching?" Arkie asked.

Outside, the bell for lunchbreak sounded. Mr Clifton stood up and had a bit of a stretch. "I want to get into my car and travel around the place. I'd like to even make it to the Northern Territory.

That's one part of Australia I've never seen."

Mr Clifton had playground duty that day, and some of the discontent followed him outside. Kylie, Rebecca and a few others marched up to him and said, "Hey Mr Clifton, why are you really leaving?"

"Yeah, is it because you're sick of us?"

"Don't you like us?"

"Are you getting married or something?"

"I reckon it's pretty slack about you leaving before the end of the year, Mr Clifton."

He sounded impatient and almost angry when he answered, "Look, I explained it all to you back inside. I told you, very honestly, that leaving was a hard decision, but one I had to make. You've been a great class to work with; don't spoil it now by coming up to me and speaking like that."

Arkie had been standing near enough to hear the course of the conversation, and had felt annoyed by Kylie's manner. *All she wants is gossip to spread around.* Arkie watched as a group of kindergarten kids ran up and commanded Mr Clifton's attention. He strolled away from them then, and Arkie walked away also, leaving Kylie, Rebecca and the others in a chattering circle.

She wandered slowly across the playground, and kids darted in front of and behind her, noisily engrossed in their own games.

"When Suzie was a schoolgirl, when Suzie was a schoolgirl," chanted two girls about Jo's age, who were facing each other and clapping their hands and knees in complicated rhythm. "When Suzie was a schoolgirl, she used to go like this: 'Miss, Miss, I can't do this, Miss Miss I can't do

127

this.'" The two of them paused as Arkie passed, and recommenced their rhyme behind her. *Kylie and I used to sing that. When Suzie was a teenager, when Suzie was a teenager, when Suzie was a teenager, she used to go like this: 'Ooh ah, I lost my bra, I left it in my boyfriend's car!' Arkie paused and grinned. We got into trouble from Mrs King once, when she heard us sing that bit.*

She passed the windows of her own classroom and stared in absently. Ian was sitting at his desk. She walked right up to the window for a closer look. He was hunched over a piece of paper or cardboard, and was drawing something very carefully with felt-tip pens. Tassels of hair hung down and obscured his face; he seemed completely oblivious to the playground noise outside.

Arkie walked around to the classroom doorway and quietly stepped inside. When she approached Ian, he went to cover up whatever he was working on, but instead sent it fluttering onto the floor. Quickly, Arkie picked it up.

"Give it here!" he said, alarmed.

"Hang on, what is it?" Arkie asked, holding it away from his grasp. It was a folded card, with a beautifully intricate abstract design on the cover. "Hey, this is great," she remarked, flipping it open.

"Give it here!" Ian repeated, standing up and trying to reach for the card.

Arkie took several steps away and read the contents. Inside, in neat printing was: GOODBYE MR CLIFTON, THANK YOU FOR BEING SUCH A GOOD TEACHER, LOVE IAN.

Ian had levelled an expectant and worried gaze at her. "Give it here," he mumbled a third time, and Arkie handed it over silently, watching as he sat down once more and resumed the abstract design on the card's front.

Love, Ian? Aloud, she told him, "That design is really great."

"Go away, Arkie please," he replied softly.

At the school disco, she found him sitting alone on one of the chairs that were positioned around the edge of the crowded playground.

"Where's Jo?" she asked.

Ian pointed out at the mob of dancing kids and teachers. In their midst, Jo and most of his year two class were laughing and bobbing about to the music that thumped and blared from the hired sound system set up on the canteen steps.

"Aren't you gonna dance, Ian?"

He shook his head.

In the girls' toilets, there were screams, shouts and the slamming of cubicle doors. On the way out Arkie paused with the congregation at the mirrors above the washbasins. Kids her age and younger combed and flicked their hair into position, whilst others dabbed at amateurishly applied makeup. She glanced at her own reflection, at the dangling leather earrings shaped like eucalyptus leaves, and the sweeping line of kohl pencil under each of her eyes.

"You look like an actress from a silent movie," had been mum's compliment.

"Hey Arkie, where's the funeral?" Sean Taylor

had yelled when Arkie and Jo had arrived at school that evening. His usual brash loudness had returned to him after having been suppressed for a time by his parents' loud and public argument in Ramsay Street. "You look like a crow, dressed in black like that, " he remarked with a snigger.

Arkie jabbed at him with a clenched fist and he shouted to a nearby teacher, "Hey, Miss Tindall, this girl's bashing me up!"

Another crowd of girls bustled into the toilets and fought for space at the mirrors. Arkie stepped outside.

There were plastic cups crushed on the ground, the smell of hot dogs that kids were buying at the canteen, and groups of supervising parents stationed around the edges of the playground. Coloured spotlights illuminated the dancers and the music was interrupted at intervals by the voice of the teacher setting up records on the sound system. Kids from her own class were standing or sitting in one corner of the playground.

"Is Mr Clifton here?"

"Not yet. He said he would be."

"He'd better."

Arkie settled amongst them and contributed the occasional comment.

"Hey, Mrs Elliot brought her husband —"

"Should see him, he's got a bigger gut than my dad has."

"Wish they'd play some decent music. Half of this is last year's stuff."

"Well go and see Mr Kennedy. He's up there playing all the records —"

"Pretending t' be Mr Cool."

"Yeah, Eric, go and give him heaps, mate."

"I will, I will."

"Hey, where's Checcutti?"

"Out dancing with Sally, of course. The girl of his dreams —"

"Huh. Last week it was Voula, I thought."

"Shut up, Lomas, I was not."

"And Adam and Sean are up in the back playground. Adam's got cigarettes —"

"What a hood."

"— they're up sharing a smoke right now."

"That's really exciting, Warren."

"Yeah Warren, we saw you puffing on a Winfield down at the skating rink last week."

"Yeah, Warren —"

"Black lungs, mate."

"Here's Adam and Sean now."

"Arkie," Kylie said in a loud voice, "go and ask Adam for a dance. He's been waiting."

Kylie and Rebecca were nearly identically dressed, and their faces were coloured with eye shadow and lip gloss. "Shut up Kylie," Arkie replied in a hostile voice, "I'm getting really sick of you saying that."

"I'm getting really sick of you saying that," Kylie mimicked.

The other kids stopped talking.

"You're always showing off," Arkie said, against the music and playground racket.

"Hey," Kylie said to the others, "You know who Arkie likes?"

"Who?" the kids chorused back.

"Ian Koh!" Kylie replied triumphantly. "He's

131

always up at Arkie's house and," she concluded with a sneer, "Arkie thinks he's really great. She told me herself."

The kids laughed and nudged each other.

"Beauty, Arkie."

"Now we know —"

"Yeah, where's Koh, anyway?"

"Let's go and drag him back here so's he and Arkie can have a dance —"

"Some friend you are," Arkie said to Kylie, taut with embarrassment. *Everybody's taking notice of Kylie.*

"Who said I'm your friend?" Kylie retorted. "I'm only looking after your stupid pets during the holidays because I'm getting paid for it —"

"Mr Clifton's here!" Adam Black interrupted and, distracted, some of the kids cheered.

Mr Clifton was edging his way past dancing children and onlooking teachers and parents. He was leading someone by the hand.

"Hey, it's Mr Clifton and his mystery girl-friend!"

"Wooo Mr Clifton, we're over here!"

"Hey, check her hair out; it's as colourful as his."

"I like her leather jacket —"

"Is it the girl your dad saw Mr Clifton with at Manly, Rebecca?"

"How should I know?"

Their faces turned away from Arkie then, as they drifted towards the teacher and his friend. Kylie and Rebecca stood to one side and began exchanging laughs and whispers, but the other

kids could be heard swapping goodnatured remarks with Mr Clifton. Arkie went to move closer
and join in, but hesitated.

"What's up with Kylie?" said someone beside
her.

Startled, Arkie swung around. Voula was next
to her, quiet and dressed as if going to church.

"I dunno," Arkie replied, "just showing off, I
guess."

"Are you going out to dance?"

Arkie shook her head. "No, not yet." She
searched the crowd on the sidelines for Ian, but
couldn't sight him.

Nearby, Mr Clifton began laughing.

He laughed a lot on the last day of school as well,
told corny jokes and made terrible puns, so that
there was a constant undercurrent of laughter and
groans from the class. What the last day of term
lacked altogether was schoolwork, because instead Mr Clifton organised cleaning and tidying.
Cupboards and desks were emptied and sorted
out, until the classroom looked like a bombsite
under assault from loads of cardboard, paper and
discarded stencils. The things from Mr Clifton's
own desk and drawers largely disappeared into
his briefcase, so that the desk itself was left
unusually bare, save for the teaching programme
in its blue folder, bequeathed to the new teacher.

"Who's our new teacher?" somone asked.

"I don't know," Mr Clifton replied with a
shrug. "Sorry."

And occasionally, someone else would say

something like, "Jeez, I wish you weren't leaving, Mr Clifton," throwing the class into momentary silence, as if waiting for their teacher to reply differently. He didn't.

"I know," was his only answer, accompanied by a thoughtful nod.

"At least we'll all be able to swap seats after the holidays," Arkie heard Kylie mumble to Rebecca.

Swap seats then, see if I care.

As morning break approached and the cleaning up activities diminished, Arkie glanced about at the walls stripped of artwork and projects; tape clinging here and there in strips and creased blobs. "What about the mice and the fish?" she asked Mr Clifton. "Are you taking those home as well?"

He tapped a hand to his forehead. "Thanks, Arkie, I almost forgot. Right, who's not going away anywhere during the holidays?"

Hands flew up.

"Sir —"

"Sir, me —"

"Mr Clifton, I'm not . . ."

Arkie had her camera in her schoolbag, and was relieved when other kids pulled Instamatics and pocket cameras from their own bags after morning break. Others produced gift-wrapped presents and Arkie felt a pang of regret that she hadn't done likewise.

"Hey, you shouldn't have . . ." Mr Clifton said, accepting the inevitable hankies, aftershave and cassettes with brave politeness. He doubled over laughing, though, when Sally DeVries and Voula carried in a goodbye cake they'd concocted at home and carefully hidden in a remote corner of the storeroom. It was lopsided, had candles, lurid green icing embedded with Smarties, and illegible tangles of words in white icing.

"It says, FAREWELL MR CLIFTON," Voula explained disdainfully, because the cake's recipient was still laughing in disbelief.

"Photos!" Mr Clifton said loudly. "I want pictures of this!" and he held the cake in front of him as kids aimed and clicked cameras. Then he adopted various other poses — standing on his desk, crucified against the blackboard, and pretending to attack Adam Black with a pointy shoe. "Don't show any of the afternoon papers that one," he remarked as the bell for lunchbreak rang, "or there'll be headlines like 'CRAZED TEACHER: LETHAL WEAPON USED ON KIDDIES'. . . ."

The class began to drift out into the playground, but Arkie remained to one side of the classroom, squinting through the viewfinder of her camera. When Mr Clifton realised she was standing there, he turned slightly and she pressed the shutter button down, capturing his oddly contemplative face against a backdrop of blurred writing on the blackboard.

After a school assembly and an afternoon of sport, a lot of the class followed Mr Clifton to his battered Datsun in the teachers' carpark. A few of them carried his boxes of stencils and books, and conversations clashed and overlapped. Beyond the school gates kids jostled at the bus stop or ran and walked along the footpath in noisy, celebratory groups.

The boxes were heaved into the back of the Datsun.

"Wish you weren't leaving, Mr Clifton," someone was still staying.

"Goodbye everyone," Mr Clifton said quietly, before getting into his car. "It's been excellent knowing you." And the last thing Arkie heard him say, before she went to find Jo and walk home, was, "Thanks for the card, Ian."

Mr Clifton said he'll come back and visit us, but I bet he won't. Arkie buried herself within the sensuous warmth of her quilt. Light from beyond the half-open door filtered into her room. *We probably won't see him again.*

". . . so they thought," came her mum's laughing voice from nearby.

Mum's and Michael's conversations were within earshot now, drifting and echoing across the hallway from where they'd often be in the evenings, seated together on the couch in the loungeroom.

They're talking about school again. Staff meetings, playground duty, table tennis in the teachers' common room. Kids sent out of class.

There was soft, comfortable laughter, voices muffled by hugging, and quiet music on the stereo.

"You're looking forward to this holiday, eh?" came Michael's voice.

"You bet I am," mum replied, "It's ages — years — since I've seen Carol for more than an hour or so. We've always had so much to talk about."

"I've only met her a few times, but you keep telling me about her."

"Mike, you cannot believe how important a friend she was when I was twelve or thirteen. I hated being sent off to boarding school, but meeting up with Carol helped me survive six years away from home —"

Their voices descended into whispers and Arkie's gaze, until then focused on the doorway, shifted to the floor near her wardrobe. There her suitcase lay open, half-packed with clothes for a holiday.

NINE

The view beyond the car window transformed itself. Arkie was curled into one corner of the back seat, so that her eyes met with the edge of the window. A framed picture beyond the glass swept by with the blur of traffic.

Gradually, the brash colour and clutter of used caryards became serene house-front gardens. Shops and overhead wires became reserves and trees, and the roadside stalls of the outer suburbs. When the Batmobile swept onto the expressway at last, everything suburban had capitulated to rock face and bushland.

Goodbye, city. See you in a fortnight.

Rain lashed against the window and wind buffeted the car. Next to where Arkie's ear was embedded in the seat's upholstery, a breeze hissed coldly through the crevice around the door. The tyres roared underneath on the wet road and music echoed from the cassette deck under the car's dashboard.

The first year we lived in Ramsay Street, Michael took us on holidays. Down the south coast, and it rained all the way.

Between herself and Jo, the back seat was piled with blankets and pillows. A colouring book and textas had fallen from the seat onto the gritty floor carpet. Jo sprawled back into his own corner of the seat gazing expressionlessly and sucking his thumb, his incessant chatter at the journey's beginning having wound down to a silence.

I was rugged up under a blanket and Jo was in his baby seat. I got carsick and mum had to change Jo's nappy parked at the side of the highway because he was stinking the car out.

Jo gazed at Arkie. She gazed back at him. The car drove on, drawing past slower cars and being overtaken by swiftly moving luxury cars. When the Batmobile drew alongside semitrailers, there was a view of wheels, undercarriage, fuel tanks, driveshafts and bullbar lights; the truckie's impassive stare down from the heights of the truck's cab. An extra rush of wind, and the truck would fade into the rear distance.

The rain continued to clatter and drum on the roof and flick itself against the windows, sounding like paper being rustled.

There was a really loud cassette on and Michael was singing to it and pulling funny faces at me in the rear view mirror.

They angle-parked in the main street of a country town and had lunch in a cafe with yellowed walls and partitions between the tables. Elderly ladies in overcoats and hats sat at other tables and spoke in guarded voices, pausing over their cups of tea to smile sweetly at Jo.

On the front seat back in the car, mum and

Michael murmured occasionally to each other. Michael studied road maps and clicked cassettes in and out of the tape player. The dashboard ashtray was jammed with Freddo Frog and Mars Bar wrappers. Mum maintained an almost trance-like gaze at the road ahead, one hand sometimes gliding from the steering wheel to the gearstick.

The road narrowed and became hillier. The towns passed were short and sudden — tanned and weatherblown, with flashes of colour on shop-fronts and service stations, a scattering of roadside litter and faded advertisement billboards at the settlement boundaries, before the wild country and bush consumed the view again. Arkie drifted off to sleep, and sometime later, blinked awake. The rain had intensified and the wind-screen wipers flicked vigorously back and forth, clearing the approaching view for split seconds. The massed clouds seemed to hang closer and closer overhead, and mountain ranges dissolved in fogs and mists. Car lights blinked their courses on the road before them.

"Are we nearly there?" Arkie asked in a raspy, walking-up voice.

"Almost," mum replied. "Another half hour or so."

"First turnoff out of town," Michael mur-mured, holding the folded map at an angle because what daylight there had been was fading. "Ten kilometres out and turn left ..."

The turnoff and final stretch of road snaked its way in narrow bitumen through open fields and across little creeks. Turning to gravel, it cut its way along a cliff edge and into hills. A wide, sand-barred river lay to one side.

"Four bridges to cross, and then the house. . ." mum said quietly, quoting written directions.

A world away from Ramsay Street and home units, the house stood utterly alone in a field bordering the road. Its woodwork was weathered brown and verandahs were populated with potted plants and old lounges. A paddock-scarred station wagon was parked haphazardly on the grass next to a fence and beside it, an identical car with no wheels and various body parts plundered. Through her car window, Arkie saw a verandah door open and two people stepping outside. It was close to night time; frogs creaked in the pad-dock grass and a fine mist of rain continued to fall. There was a vague hint of chimney smoke in the air, and the odour of animals somewhere nearby. Arkie, Jo, mum and Michael freed themselves of the car and walked towards the house.

The conversation rushed forth then, a barrage of laughter, greetings and talk. In the half-light, Arkie took in the faces at the doorway. *Carol looks almost exactly the same as she does in those pictures mum has of them at high school. Skinny. Glasses. Smiling.*

"Arkie, you and Jo seem so tall all of a sudden," Carol said. She had dark eyes, a puckish smile and a thick plait of dark brown hair.

"It's twelve months since you saw them last, Carol."

"A year? That time's really gone, hasn't it?"

"Take yourselves into the loungeroom," John

told them. "The fire's going." He clumped after them in his farmer's corduroys and boots, clutching in one arm a dark-haired, dark-eyed toddler. Rhys was taking quick, shy glances at the newcomers and then burying his face in the shelter of his father's shoulder. "How many hours were you on the road?" John asked.

"Nine," mum replied, "and it rained all the way."

Arkie stretched her hands and arms above and behind her, easing off the hours of restraint in the car. Jo stood beside her at the loungeroom fireplace, gazing tiredly about. "John looks like a bushranger with that big beard," he murmured to her.

Arkie nodded and said nothing, as the adults' conversation continued around them. The house's inside walls were the same dark brown as those outside, lending the rooms shadow and a dim light. There was a smell of timber, candle wax, incense and something cooking on the wood stove in the kitchen; the faint voice of a newsreader on the old valve radio that sat in a corner of the loungeroom.

Carol and mum have been friends for... almost twenty years. It'd be amazing knowing someone that long.

Jo set off with mum and Michael to explore the house.

"You coming, Arkie?"

"Not yet. I'll look later."

What would it be like knowing Kylie that long? What would it be like when we're thirty or thirty-one? What would we talk about? Dance

142

steps. Husbands, because she'll be married by then. Not me. I'll be living in a house like this.

Arkie glanced at the crackling fire behind her and the clutter of books and ornaments on the mantlepiece. In her mind, she summed up the last few weeks of school, and sighed with disappointment and sadness. *But I guess me and Kylie aren't friends any more.*

Jo came bounding back into the loungeroom. "Arkie, Arkie, guess what!"

"What?"

"John's got a trail bike, and Michael said he'll take me riding. And there's chickens and pet sheep in the backyard and..." He rattled off further excitements. Rhys toddled into the loungeroom and smiled at them cautiously, and then the adults returned, still busy with their conversations. Mum and Carol were hugging each other and laughing.

When Arkie woke the next morning, there was perfect stillness and sunshine spilling in onto the floorboards. The bed she was in sagged in the middle like a canyon between mountains, and squeaked whenever she shifted her weight. In the room's other bed lay Jo, breathing in heavy sleep. The window revealed a tangle of garden outside, and when she eased herself into a sitting position Arkie could see spiderwebs and leaves dripping with the night's rain, a dangling makeshift clothesline hung with wet nappies and a group of cows beyond a wire fence, moving about and chewing on mouthfuls of grass. The bedroom door was silently pushed open then, and one of the household cats walked in, flopped down onto the floor where the warm light was, and began lazily and erratically to wash itself. Next to the bed was a box of books, and Arkie leant over and pulled several out. She lay back and looked through them until the rest of the house began to wake.

Each morning Arkie woke to the brief period of silence and the sight outside of grazing cows and water birds strutting through the paddocks. She became used to the rising and familiar pattern of noises, the sheep in the yard bleating and the crack, thud from outside as John cut and split the day's supply of firewood. She became used to heating up water for the bucket shower in the draughty bathroom and to the outside toilet with its collection of *Phantom* comics and back issues of *The Bulletin*. Each frosty morning, she and Jo huddled around the wood stove in the kitchen eating bowls of porridge, while the sheep congregated at the back door, noisily clamouring for breadcrusts. For the first few days, she sat herself on one of the verandah couches and worked her way through some of the books from her bedroom. From around the house came the sounds of the adults' voices engaged in perpetual story-telling and conversation, records on the loungeroom stereo. Jo and Rhys ran and wandered endlessly around the home paddocks and explored the tiny creek that cut along one boundary fence. Minor breezes set the washing flapping on the wire clothesline, and bird calls rang out. The odd moments of quiet made Arkie look up from her reading and gaze about, and gradually she picked out old fence lines in the near distance and the odd brick pile of building ruins.

"There was a town here once," Carol said, pointing to the view that was empty of almost anything created by human hands. She looked at Arkie, and then traced a pointed finger along the line of dirt road that passed the front paddock. "Houses. Two pubs, a post office. If you were to go down and look, the foundations are still quite clear in places. There was a school, too."

"What happened?" Arkie asked.

"Several years of drought. Children grew up, left school and left the district. Lure of the big city and all that. The school had to close and people just moved away . . . the houses were mostly demolished by farmers who wanted grazing space. This house survived."

"Who lived here before you?"

"A young couple had it built and moved here after their honeymoon. Four years later, the wife died in childbirth."

"That's sad."

"Mm. The husband moved away after that, and the house sat empty for almost fifty years."

"Wow."

"Well, not quite, I guess. Itinerant workers stayed here from time to time. And it was used to store hay bales in. John and I heard about it being on the market and we raised the cash to buy it. We were very lucky, really."

Someone else's cows grazed at random in the paddock across the road, trampling through grass that Arkie realised must once have been people's yards and a school's playground.

"There was a whole town down there?" she said.

Carol nodded. "I can even show you what it used to look like," she answered, and ducked inside to delve through the loungeroom bookshelves. She returned with a plain yellow volume. "A history of the local area I found gathering dust in the general store in town," she said, thumbing through the pages. "Here it is."

The reproduced photo showed a wider road lined with trees and low slab buildings. There were drays, traps and horses parked at odd angles, children in hats and black stockings, women with bonnets and men with beards and waistcoats.

Impressed, Arkie blinked from the view to the photo and back again. "It looked really nice," she said. "It looks nice now too, but..."

"And here's this house," Carol went on, turning several pages.

Arkie looked. The house in the photo was fresher, newer and surrounded by garden and trees. A path led down to a painted gate and fence. At the gate, a young couple in dapper clothes posed beside a running-boarded car. To one side was a tennis court.

"A tennis court!" Arkie exclaimed. "There was a tennis court here?"

Wherever it had been was now the same tussocked grass that filled the rest of the paddock. The gate and fences, the garden likewise, were nowhere to be seen.

146

"What happened to it all?"

Carol shrugged. "The farmer from the next property was leasing this block for his cows and needed more grazing space. So he came in with a bulldozer and flattened everything except the house."

"Stupid —" Arkie said. Only a few gnarled lemon trees beside the house had survived the onslaught, a greedy quest for cattle feed.

Carol gave her the book to look through, and for a moment remained at the verandah railing. "You're so much like your mum, Arkie."

"I look a lot like my dad."

"No, I mean you're the same person all over again. You speak and think the way I remember Susan when she was your age."

"I'm no good at music the way mum was. And is."

"I hear you're good at photography."

"Oh, no . . . I dunno. My first roll of film's still in the camera."

Later that day, Arkie laced up her runners, swung the camera onto one shoulder and pocketed an apple before setting off outdoors.

John and Michael had spent the morning repairing fences, but had now joined Carol and mum on the front verandah. Their conversation was being animated somewhat, Arkie thought tolerantly, by the cask of wine that sat on the floorboards between their feet.

". . . Well, Carol and I," mum was starting. She burst out laughing, and then, composing herself, she tried again. "Carol and I were once suspended from school for two weeks —"

"What?" Michael and John chorused. "How come?"

"For smoking," Carol answered, "behind the toilets."

"Ooh ah," Michael and John chorused again.

"The nuns were livid. Nicotine stains on our school gloves, senior prefects and all. They confiscated our cigarettes and phoned our mothers."

"Broke our parents' hearts, we did —"

"Well, for a little while, anyway. And then another time, we wagged school to go to a rock concert —"

"I'm going out," Arkie said loudly as she passed the verandah, "exploring."

Jo and Rhys were at the far end of the verandah playing demolition derby with toy cars. "Can I come too?" Jo asked.

Arkie groaned. "No, stay here. Leave me in peace."

"Stay here, Jo," mum said. To Arkie, she inquired, "Where exactly are you going?"

Arkie pointed across the paddock. "I'm going t' climb the hill across the road and see what the view's like."

"Be back by five then. Don't wander any further than the hill and don't get yourself lost. We might not be in any shape to come and rescue you."

Arkie set off across the paddock with gleeful energy.

Behind her, Jo called out, "Well, I'm staying

here with Michael. He might take me for a ride around the paddock on John's trail bike —"

The adults were laughing again.

Once, someone played tennis here. Arkie kicked at the passing ground with one foot to see if there was any telltale orange sand. *Nothing.* Just grass, dirt and pebbles.

The house and the voices diminished behind her. Pushing a barbed wire strand down with one hand, she negotiated the fence and stepped out onto the road. There was no traffic to look out for; the only vehicle that day had been the mail car. Besides, the noise of any car would be heard or seen from a great distance, as quiet rumble or maybe a rising veil of dust in dry weather. She turned around, unlatched the camera case and took a photo of the house.

There was another fence across the road and a paddock beyond, nibbled to ground level by cows. It might have looked almost like a suburban lawn, except that it was bumpy and spotted with animal droppings. A grove of green and drooping trees indicated the creek that ran from the rickety bridge out on the road. The bank was muddied and the creek had broken into several courses with the rain, running around little islands of grass and trees before continuing on its way into the distance. The water babbled clear, over pebbles. In the bushes to one side, something scuttled away.

A rabbit. It's just me and the rabbits out here.

The mountain stood yawning before her, trees and rocks reaching up a slope. Little paths, defined at intervals by burrowed holes, zigzagged

149

back and forth towards the top. With resolve, Arkie set off up the nearest one.

The climb was steep, like climbing the hill in Ramsay Street. A trick of perception had made it look easier and shorter than it really was and at the top finally, she sat down. Her brow oozed sweat and her heart was thumping.

She took in the view. The house sat distant in its paddock, its tin roof rusty and the cars parked to one side like toys. There was a suggestion of movement from the figures on one verandah, but no sound of their conversations. Several kilometres away to either side were the neighbouring houses, with their roofs and gaggles of sheds visible. Beyond that, infinite trees and bush.

The hilltop was almost clear, save for a few gums and bushes. Ant hills occupied the open spaces of dirt and insects busied themselves on the ground near Arkie's feet. She stood up, moved away and turned to face endless hills stretching towards the horizon. One adjacent hill was far rockier than its neighbours and with a start, she noticed what looked like a series of crevices — maybe caves — in one rock wall.

Finding an animal track that appeared to veer down towards this rock face, she set off once more. Kangaroos on the slope froze momentarily and then bounded away across the open gap of ground between the hills. Her feet and legs growing accustomed to the hike, Arkie fell into a regular stride, feeling almost as though she might be able to make it absolutely anywhere in the space of an afternoon.

*Where's the nearest town? Where's the nearest
house this side of the hill?*

Climbing a minor rise, the rocky crevices fell
from view and it was then that she heard the
noise. It was a clinking noise, totally at odds
with the surroundings, and for a moment her ears
fought to find the exact direction from which it
came.

Coming to the top of the rise and looking down
at the pasture below, she saw three figures. Two
were walking ahead and a third was running to
catch up, the clinking noise seeming to fit the
rhythm of the one running. They were all children,
Arkie's age and younger, and quickly she dropped
to her knees to avoid being seen. They were quite a
distance away, too distant for Arkie to tell whether
they were boys or girls, and seemed to be heading
towards the rock face with its crevices.

"Where have they come from?" she said to
herself in a low voice, staring down at the ground
beneath her knees. Insects clambered over grass
shoots, yellow pebbles and white quartz. There
was glare from the half-hearted sun. Overhead,
sulphur-crested cockatoos dipped out of the sky,
squawking discordantly, swooping over to a
nearby tree and then making their noisy way to
another. Shattering the silence every few minutes,
they squawked and changed trees until they'd
made their way across the valley to the blur of
bush on another mountain, and their sounds were
echoes.

When Arkie looked over to where the three
children were, it was to see them climbing
amongst the rocks and boulders at the base of the

creviced hill. One of them seemed to be looking around , searching the valley and hills for signs of life.

Do they know I'm here?

Intrigued by the apparent furtiveness of their movements, she watched as the three of them came not to the largest of the crevices, but to the smallest. And one by one they crawled into its shadowed entrance.

For the first time since Arkie had left the house, she glanced at her watch, and the digital numbers blinked from minute to minute, silently marking the next quarter of an hour. She waited and watched for the three children to reappear. She tried finding a way to move closer to where they were, but the ground in between offered no hiding places.

At last, they reappeared. Crawling out of the crevice on their hands and knees, the three children retraced their steps down amongst the rocks to the grassy paddocks below. Two of them sprinted ahead, and as the third ran to catch up, the odd clinking sound echoed starkly again.

Arkie frowned, puzzled.

Little by little, the three figures diminished. They climbed a slope to Arkie's left and disappeared from view. She took a heavy breath, checked to see that they hadn't reappeared, and stood up. White clouds hung above like wisps of cotton wool and sunlight held the landscape in unhazed clarity. A breeze picked up, ruffling grass stalks and rattling leaves in box trees. Arkie jogged, walked and jogged from point to point down the slope.

Coming to the rocks at the base of the hillside, she negotiated their jagged edges and smooth surfaces until she met with breeze of cold air at the entrance to the smallest of the crevices. The other two, she'd noted, were merely indents in the rock that stretched only a couple of metres into the cliff face, but this particular crevice had more depth — an actual interior that had not been visible at first. Briefly, she looked back to where she had hidden and waited — distant now — and then around at the quiet hills. There was stillness and isolation, no-one and nothing, and she knelt down on the dirt to negotiate the entrance. *Urk. Hope there're no spiders or snakes.* But all she could see were scuffmarks and footprints on the ground around her. Ducking her head to avoid a jutting edge of rock, she crawled through the gap.

The light within was not darkened, merely dimmed, because along one edge of the crevice's interior was a handspan's width between two boulders and the sunlight filtered in onto a dirt floor and a low-ceilinged space that was about the size of a garden toolshed.

Arkie blinked and gaped.

Nothing had prepared her for what was here. On a rocky shelf, a little above the floor, was a collection of things. No, not things, but possessions. *Someone's belongings.*

There was a pair of tall black leather boots, a pair of large black leather gloves, a pair of broken sunglasses, a motorcyclist's crash helmet — old fashioned, but plastered with newish stickers — a man's watch, a pair of dusty jeans, and a photograph.

In awe, she stared at it all, glancing quickly behind (was someone there? no) and then turning to pick the photograph up. It was a small Polaroid shot, slipped into a perspex frame. Holding it to the light, Arkie saw a man with laughing eyes, a huge black beard and a ponytail of black hair. He was wearing the gloves and helmet and sitting astride a fairly old-looking motorbike. He wasn't the only one in the photograph, either. Perched on the handlebars, the fuel tank, the cushion seat at the bike's rear, and on the motorcyclist's lap, were four small boys — two toddlers, a preschooler and another about Jo's age. The bike and its occupants leant lazily on a driveway somewhere. The photo's colours were a bit faded. *And who are they? There's nothing written on the back to say.*

She set the photo down once more and stared at the collection again, uncomprehending. She moved around the rocky space, head bent to avoid overhanging rock and mud insect nests that clung like blisters to the roof. Her footprints mingling with the others on the floor, she unhitched the camera and clicked the lens adjustments around until the light reading seemed right. Facing the rock shelf with its museum of objects, she pressed the shutter button and turned to leave.

About to kneel down for the crawl back to the outside, Arkie stopped to pick up another photograph that lay curled up and almost out of sight under a granite overhang. This photo was frameless, bent and dustier than the first; black and white, a baby picture this time. A child with sparse black hair, large dark eyes and a gummy grin stared up at whoever had been the photographer. In neat, adult handwriting on the back was *Tony Arcana, ten months.*

The sunlight, August and lukewarm, made her squint when she'd taken the half-dozen crawls outside. Blinking, she took in the unchanged landscape and the faraway squawks of cockatoos. She looked down at the photo still in her hand, and on impulse slipped it into her pocket.

A sense of some kind of tragedy followed her home.

Her mum was seated crosslegged on the ground in front of the house, an exercise book balanced in her lap. Pen poised, she looked up. "So how was the exploring?"

Arkie looked down at the open exercise book, at lines of writing in her mum's script. Some bits were crossed out. *Right in this spot, there used to be a garden.* "Alright," she answered. "What are you doing?"

"What am I doing? I'm writing lyrics. Words to go with music." She looked up at Arkie, deeply thoughtful. "I haven't written words to go with music for years and years. Something made me start again."

"So what did you see out there today?" John asked, as all of them sat around the large table in the kitchen that night. There was a clutter of crockery, cutlery and one or two winecasks. "Any wildlife? Anything exciting?" He stroked his beard with scratched, work-marked hands.

Arkie shrugged. "Ants, spiders, sulphur-crested cockatoos, six kangaroos —"

"Riding the trail bike was good fun," Jo interrupted.

The photo sat concealed in Arkie's jacket pocket. "— and three kids," she concluded.

"As in children?" Carol asked from her side of the table. Rhys was beside her in a high chair, dribbling mashed something down his chin.

Arkie nodded a reply.

"Where did you see them?" Carol added.

"The other side of the hill," Arkie said, feeling sure that everyone could see the stiff rectangle of photo in her pocket. "Three boys, I think. Just walking around."

Carol and John exchanged glances. John said, "Sounds like the Arcanas out strolling about."

"Who?" Arkie quickly asked, because the name sounded familiar.

"Neighbours," John answered, pouring himself another glass of wine and topping up Michael's glass as well. "Jean Arcana lives down the road, a gate about two kilometres away. She has five sons —"

"Five!" mum exclaimed. "Wow, one is enough."

"Stop joking, mum," Jo told her seriously.

John continued, "— five sons aged from, what . . . ? Three up to twelve."

"When they were walking along," Arkie said cautiously, not wanting to reveal too much of what she'd seen that afternoon, "there was this clinking noise."

Carol smirked and nodded. "Cowbells."

"Huh?"

"Cowbells. The three younger Arcanas each have a cowbell around their neck on a string, so their mother can keep track of where they are —"

"Great idea," mum said with strange emphasis, looking with raised eyes in Jo's direction. He was too busy laughing at Rhys's eating habits.

"They've lived here five years," John said. "I reckon they know the hills and creeks around these parts like the backs of their hands."

"They keep to themselves a lot at school, from what we hear," Carol added. "They're really. . . solitary. A bit like their mother. The father was killed on a motorbike two, no, over three years ago. A bit before the youngest child was born."

"Poor kids," said mum.

So that's it. All the motorcycle stuff and the photos.

"Poor lady," said Michael. "All those kids by herself?"

Carol nodded. "Actually, she's quite amazing. We could probably pay her a call tomorrow; she likes visitors, and the boys might be interested in meeting Arkie and Jo."

"Didn't you meet them today?" Michael asked Arkie, suddenly puzzled.

She shook her head. "They were a long way away. I just watched them for a while." *And stole their photograph.*

"Speaking of getting out and about," John said, "there's a dance on Saturday night. There's a little village on a hilltop about thirty kilometres away, and the community group there stages dances once a month."

"What kind of dance?" Arkie asked.

"People flock from out of the valleys, forests and other places —"

"What kind of dance?" Arkie repeated.

157

John shrugged. "Rock and roll. Good, classic bop-till-you-drop stuff. Very intellectual. The band's great, besides. Why d'you ask?"

Arkie made a face. "Last year we learnt things at school like the Barn Dance and Canadian Threestep. Really daggy stuff. I was hoping it wasn't going to be, you know, like that." *Or like the school disco. That wasn't a lot of fun at all.*

TEN

Letterboxes were ranged together, at intervals along the road. They were paint, feed and dairy drums with family names marked on their sides. They sat nailed to posts at the beginnings of tracks that tumbled away into bushland.

"Where do all the roads go?" Jo asked.

"Over the hills and far away," Carol answered in a lilting voice, clunking the gear lever down as the old Falcon wagon banged and clattered over rubble and bumps, "to people's houses. To farms and properties."

There was dust swirling around the car's interior, a contrast to the road outside that remained rain-damp. Everything — dashboard, seats, door handles — had a film of dirt over it. There were leaves caught in the air vents next to the steering wheel and what Arkie, Jo and Rhys were sitting on in the back felt more like a trampoline than a seat.

"It smells funny back here," Jo remarked, and whispered to Arkie, "like poo."

"Maybe Rhys needs a nappy change," mum turned around and said.

"No, it's more like . . . you know, cows."

Carol smirked. "John and I went around the paddocks last week after horse manure for the vegie patch. We had it loaded in the back there; maybe it's traces of that you can smell."

Arkie and Jo made vomiting noises, looked at each other and laughed.

"You'd never mistake them for country kids, would you?" mum said to Carol.

"What's this place we're going to?" Arkie asked.

"Wait and see," Carol replied, and the car lurched onto a sealed road surface. "The Arcanas live in the most amazing house you've ever laid eyes on."

"What's it look like?"

"Wait and see."

"Come on, give us a clue."

"Alright. It's got walls and windows. And it's amazing."

"Aw..."

The car bounced off the brief dose of proper road and down a side track between trees. Then the track divided itself into several more sets of tyre paths that led away to unknown destinations. Carol drove the Falcon down one of them.

"We're doubling back, almost," she said. "Where we'll wind up isn't all that far from home."

The car stopped on an open rise.

"I'll get it," said Jo quickly, and leapt out of the car to undo the steel and wire gate that stood before them. A rusted wire fence stretched away to either side, and there was no sign of a house, just the meandering dirt driveway that disappeared from view over the first grassy rise.

"Where's the house?" Jo called after them. No reply. He heaved the gate shut, slipped the chain and catch back over the post hook and ran to the car. They drove on along the track, beneath clustered gum trees, over two causeways and across low-running creek beds. Each small rise they crossed revealed another range of grey-green hills in the distance.

"This is the longest driveway I've ever seen," Arkie mumbled, and peered through the bug-smeared windscreen for a glimpse of the house.

Suddenly it came into view, and what they saw was no ordinary house at all, but a doubledecker bus planted in the middle of a cleared square of ground. The windows that existed were curtained; others that had existed were now aluminium wall. A chimney poked through the roof, and around the perimeter of the bus was a lean-to verandah, punctuated at one end by an open shed, where a collection of children's pushbikes and dinkies sat piled. The bus's paintwork was faded green and brown, and the destination board read "Home".

"Wow," Jo managed to say, voicing Arkie's and mum's amazement as well.

Next to the bus was parked a car, another paddock-scarred station wagon with missing hubcaps and bug-spattered paintwork. There were toys scattered around the yard and a clothesline full of washing. At one of the bus windows, a curtain was pulled aside and two small faces peered out, and it was then that Arkie felt a rush of apprehension. *Supposing they saw me yesterday. Maybe they've been back to their cave and found the photo missing —*

"Morgan, Ben, Anton, Rowan, Christy," Jean Arcana said in the kitchen of her bus-house, introducing each of her children, from the oldest down to the youngest. Jean was dressed in baggy shorts and a frayed sloppy joe with *University of New England* printed on the front. She had dark hair and dark skin; her children shared her Mediterranean complexion and looks exactly. Later, Jo said to Arkie, "They look like Ian," and he was right, because they had the same tassels of dark hair and the same large nervous eyes. They regarded Arkie and Jo now with nods and shy glances, and barely spoke.

"Why don't you show Arkie and Jo around?" Jean Arcana asked the older boys in a quiet voice, and the boys led Arkie and Jo outside. Behind them, she asked mum, "What d'you do down in the city?"

"I'm a high school music teacher," mum replied.

Jean Arcana laughed softly. "That must take a bit of courage —"

Chairs were moved around on the bus floor as the three women settled themselves around a table. Arkie had paused at the bus doorway to listen, but switched her attention to the scene outside.

"Hey, can I have a go on one of your bikes?" Jo asked enthusiastically and without reserve. He,

162

Ben and Anton trooped off purposefully towards the shed. The two youngest boys remained near Arkie and gazed seriously up at her. When she smiled back at them, not really knowing what to say, they took refuge next to their eldest brother. Around their necks, she noted, were small brass bells hung on plaited leather cord.

The eldest boy, Morgan, was looking at Arkie steadily, but turned away slightly when she returned his stare. At first, he seemed reluctant to say anything at all, concentrating his attention on his brothers and then on Rhys, who was negotiating the steps out of the bus. "What class are you in at school?" he asked her finally.

Arkie was surprised at the sound of his voice, a shy and rasping near-whisper. She'd also been occupied matching the Arcanas' faces with those in the colour photograph in the rock crevice. *On that motorbike with their dad, smiling and looking happy.* At last, she answered, "Sixth."

His voice was as solemn as his mother's. "Yeah, me too."

"It's nice around here," she said. "Have you explored much of it?"

"A lot of it," he replied steadily. "Why?"

Arkie shrugged. "Just wondered."

"I guess you like the city better than the country. Things to do and see."

She slowly shook her head. "I used to like the city, but not any more, really. We've got a good house, but. The only backyard in the whole street, nearly. Kids come up to our place to play games and stuff, because they all live in home units. We can keep pets and they can't —" *I'm talking too much, he doesn't like it.*

But Morgan Arcana asked, "What sort of pets?"

"A cat. A lazy, greedy one called Goodvibes. And a crazy dog called Headley."

"Called what?"

"He's got a big head. Headley. He's Michael's dog, really." And she added, unwillingly yet needing to explain, "Michael's our stepfather." *Stepfather's a weird thing to call Michael.*

Morgan nodded. Next to the bus was a plank propped on two old milk churns, and he sat down. One younger brother had wandered off, cowbell tinkling, to play somewhere with Rhys, but Christy, the littlest brother, remained and climbed onto Morgan's lap. Jo and the two other boys were racing and rattling around the yard on pushbikes, having turns at locking back wheels and skidding. Over in one corner of the yard were several hexagonal wire enclosures containing hens, guinea fowl and geese.

Morgan pointed at them and said, "Those are our pets. If we had a dog or a cat up here, the wildlife'd get killed off."

He talks like an adult.

With a nod, Arkie indicated the bus. "I like this. It'd be great to live in."

"They used to have these sort of buses in Sydney, years ago. Our dad bought it from someone and fixed it up so we could live in it."

"Does it still work?"

164

"Mum starts it up every few weeks. She's good with engines and things."

He's not going to say anything about his father. "Your dad must have been pretty clever," said Arkie with an effort.

Morgan turned and seemed to look at her a long time, before he said in a quiet voice, "He was."

Arkie shifted uncomfortably and tried to concentrate on the endless hills and bush that lay beyond the yard. *I like being here. It's like somewhere I've always wanted to live but've never seen before.* She glanced at Morgan, who was stroking his little brother's back and staring at nothing in particular. Quickly, she speculated on the Arcanas' life at school. *I reckon Morgan would take really good care of his brothers.* She let images of Ramsay Street flash through her mind. *What sort of a holiday is Ian having? Brothers and sisters is what he should have had, but he's only got himself, hasn't he?*

"Can I take a photo of you?" she asked Morgan, and felt embarrassed by the curious look he gave her. "You and your brothers, I mean."

"What for?"

"I like taking photos of people. I've got a camera in the car."

She returned with the Voigtlander, and with some persuasion the five brothers, together with Jo and Rhys, collected themselves beside the bus and stared at Arkie as she fiddled with the camera. From within the bus came the laughing voices of mum, Jean Arcana and Carol. There were low calls

165

from the birds in their enclosures and a slight breeze that ruffled Arkie's cropped hair. She stared through the viewfinder at the seven faces looking back at her, Jo with his usual silly grin and Rhys with a thumb in his mouth. The five Arcana boys stood close together. *I'm sorry I've got your photo, but I'm only borrowing it.* Slowly, she pressed the shutter button.

Morgan didn't say anything more about his dad. How old was he when he died? In that colour photo, he didn't look any older than Michael.

The car's bumpy progress jolted Arkie's concentration, and she heaved herself into a more comfortable position, sitting as she was in the very back of Carol and John's station wagon. Quickly, she felt to make sure the blanket was still underneath her. *Hope I don't get to this dance smelling like horse manure. Yuk.* Everybody — Carol, John, Rhys, mum, Michael and Jo — were crammed into the car, and as they drove through the darkness, the adults speculated about the dance, in bursts of bright conversation.

It'd be sad having someone die when they're so young. Morgan and his mum and brothers still look like they're really sad about it.

The car forged a corridor of sweeping light as it drove into the night. Some distance ahead were the winking tail lights of another car, weaving its own way along and around the contours of the road. The silhouettes beyond the car windows were of guideposts, hills, and the towering trees of untouched forests. The hills had been distant at first, but now they began to rear up on either side of the road, as the contours became the twists and contortions of a steep climb.

But Christy didn't even know his dad, because he was born after the motorbike accident.

The stars and moon shone white and distinct against the black sky, but no light seemed to reach the ground they passed. Everything about was darkly indistinct, shielded and swallowed by the rise of mountains into which the car had ventured.

Like our dad hardly knows Jo. Or me.

The road levelled and straightened slightly as the landscape around opened up. If a few darkened houses could be called a town, that was it, because they were passed by in a matter of seconds. Forest consumed the view again for several minutes, until suddenly there was a glimmer of light that didn't belong to the car travelling ahead, but to a building.

It was a large weatherboard hall, crouched in a clearing and surrounded by trees. John bounced the station wagon off the road, across a ditch and into a paddock beside the building, where maybe thirty other cars were parked. There were people milling around the doors to the hall, and a few children chasing each other around in the semi-darkness.

"Well!" John announced, "we're here!"

Slamming the car doors shut behind them, they all stepped out into the cold night air. Jo was blinking his eyes and staring dreamily about; Arkie realised only then that he'd been asleep in the car.

"What do you —" Michael started to ask, but his query was cut short by the thump-thump of a drum kit and the sudden roar of electric instruments. At that moment, the entire building started vibrating to dozens of jumping, dancing feet and a voice sailed forth with the music from the open, illuminated entrance.

Mum was saying, "Now please stay with us, you two. Don't just go wandering off," but Jo had suddenly found himself full of energy and was sprinting towards the hall entrance.

This is amazing, here in the middle of nowhere, a noisy band and stacks of people. Arkie followed the others inside, feeling the further onslaught of music noise, and the sounds and smells of people — vague gusts of scent, alcohol, and for one moment, food. They walked along the boundary of the dance floor, passing a doorway to a side room where people were setting out food on large tables — pastries, dips and flat bread, spinach pies and more. Ahead, Michael made some wisecrack and mum doubled over with laughter. John had an armful of blankets and Carol carried Rhys, who was still asleep despite the racket around him. People around were shouting to each other over the din of the music, and the centre floor was crammed with people of all ages, some in outlandish masquerade dress, others in more anonymous garb. The lighting from the stage occasionally caught their faces in washes of colour. There were chairs around the sides of the hall, and more clustered at the back, occupied by adults watching the dancing and by children asleep under jackets and blankets. Carol laid Rhys across two chairs and carefully covered him.

"Come on, Fred Astaire!" mum called to Michael, and led him onto the dance floor.

Arkie looked at Carol and said, "I'll keep an eye on Rhys for a while, if you like," because she thought John and Carol might want to go and dance as well. They nodded gratefully to her.

She settled on a chair next to Rhys. Beside her, Jo stood on a chair for a better view, and was quietly transfixed.

Where are mum and Michael? Arkie stood up on her own chair. Across a sea of bobbing heads she sighted them, right at the front where the band were sweating it out under stage lights. *Checking out the band, of course, like mum always wants to do.*

The music finished, to cheers and applause, as mum and Michael worked their way back to where Arkie, Jo and Rhys were.

"Exhausting!" John exclaimed, as he and Carol also returned.

Mum picked Jo off his seat. "Come on, young man, show me your style," she said, and led him out amongst the dancers.

The band rasped and thumped into a new song. "Care for a waltz?" Michael shouted to Arkie.

She rolled her eyes and wrinkled her nose goodnaturedly at him, so that he laughed. They edged onto the dance floor and worked their way then amongst dancing couples, until they found a vacant patch.

There were other children dancing, too, some moving with practised ease, others leaping and hopping around in complete contradiction to the music's beat. Arkie turned slightly and found her mother and Jo nearby, mum with her usual seriousness and involvement, but Jo blatantly showing off. *Being a complete idiot, like he goes when nan puts those Mantovani records on at her place.*

Side step, side step, turn, shake. Abruptly, she realised her dance routine had originated one Sunday morning in Kylie's flat, and she altered her pattern of movement so that it became more like Michael's quirky jiving. Half-nervously, she glanced about, feeling as though she was being watched, but the people around her were concerned with their own enjoyment.

At the interval, she queued up for a helping of food, and then stepped outside to eat. Behind her in the hall was the continuing din of voices; here outside the vague strains of night insects and a group of children playing a relentless game of chasings amongst the parked cars. Her mum was sitting at the base of the entrance steps, a plate of food balanced in her lap.

"Thought I saw you come out here," Arkie said, sitting down also.

"Mm," mum replied, sipping from a plastic cup of wine she'd bought inside. "Where's Jo?"

"In with Michael and Carol and John," Arkie replied, and began eating. After a few minutes, she became aware that her mother was not so much eating as staring into space. "What's wrong, mum?" she asked.

"Nothing's wrong. I'm just thinking."

"What about?"

"About music."

"What, the stuff you've been writing in that exercise book? The words?"

Mum shrugged. "That too. I've mainly been thinking about those boxes and boxes of tapes at home, the music I've been recording since the year dot. I've been thinking about what a good time I had when I was nineteen, at teachers' college, and playing in a band."

"Why?"

Mum picked a slice of spinach pie from her paper plate and took a few mouthfuls. Behind them in the hall a voice boomed "GOOD EVENING, EVERYBODY" over a microphone, and started rattling off a series of community announcements.

Mum took another sip of wine, creased her mouth thoughtfully and said, "One of the English teachers at school — Alan Kesey, who's been to our place once or twice — has had a band together for a year or so now, and they've started playing in some of the local pubs." She paused and sighed. "The point is —" she hesitated again and shrugged a little self-consciously, "— he wants me to join."

Arkie broke into a surprised smile. "Hey mum, that's great."

"You think so?"

"Yeah. Really."

"If I join, it means practising a couple of nights a week. And working Friday and Saturday nights. I've talked to Michael about it —"

"What did he say?"

It was mum's turn to smile, then. "He said, 'Go on. Join.' So when school starts back again, I think I'm saying yes to Alan Kesey."

"That's great. All that stuff you've got taped —"

"But Alan's band mostly play other people's songs."

"Well, that's alright." She looked at mum and smirked. "What'll nan think when she hears?"

Mum pulled a face. "Agh. I can't begin to imagine." She clasped a hand around Arkie's shouder and they huddled together.

"It's freezing around here," mum said softly. Her voice was right next to Arkie's face.

"Mum?"

"Yeah?"

A pause. "Are you and Michael ever going to have a baby?"

There was a quiet laugh. "Have you been thinking about that?"

Arkie shrugged. "I think about it sometimes, that's all."

Her mum sighed. "I think about it, too, and so does Michael. It'd be strange having a baby around after all this time —"

"Nappies all over the place. Prams and squeaky toys," Arkie commented.

Her mum giggled and tossed her head back, staring up at the dark sky. "I don't know, Arkie," she said, smiling, but seriously. "That's something we'll all have to wait and see about."

In the hall, there were random guitar notes and tentative tapping on the drum kit, as the musicians resumed their places.

"Come on," mum said, standing up. "Let's get back inside where it's warm."

Arkie found her way back to where she'd been sitting between Jo and Rhys, whilst the four adults rejoined the dancing crowd. Rhys was still fast asleep under blankets and gradually, Arkie felt Jo's weight leaning against her as he fell asleep also. She gazed into the crowd.

I have to ask if we can visit the Arcanas again. I have to do some more exploring. I have to —

She felt her eyes dropping closed.

An unknown time later, with the sounds of voices and cars being started, she felt herself being carried. *It's Michael carrying me.* The station wagon doors were opened. "Sweet dreams," Michael whispered, lying her down in the back and covering her with a blanket.

This is like being five or six years old again.

In the cold still of early morning, they arrived back at the house. Woken, Arkie and Jo managed to wander indoors and mum followed them into the spare room, turned back the covers on both beds and sat down to help Jo out of his sneakers. His eyes were almost closed again and he wavered slowly from side to side, trying to unbutton a zip-up jacket and wondering grumpily why it would not undo.

Arkie bundled herself gratefully under blankets and covers, and listened as mum tucked Jo into bed and whispered him goodnight.

Her voice was next to Arkie then. "Did you have a good time?" she asked quietly.

Arkie raised her face above the blankets and nodded. "Where's Michael?"

"In the car, asleep. I'll have to go and wake him. Listen, tell Jo we're sleeping in tomorrow. He is not to come bursting in to our room at six am, because if he does, I will personally tie him to the nearest gum-tree or feed him to the sheep or something."

They smiled at each other, sleepy eyes rolling at the horrors of life with Jo. "See you in the morning," mum whispered, "late," and kissed Arkie on the cheek.

The light went off and the door clicked closed. She lay in the darkness listening to various sets of footsteps around the house, car doors being closed, water running in the bathroom and lights being turned off. Mum, Carol and John were talking and Michael's voice was somewhere too, mumbling and then laughing quietly.

Our holiday's half over.

She breathed in the house smells of timber, dust and age; heard the cows in the back paddock rustling through the grass.

Abruptly and clearly, Jo's voice rang out in the darkness. "You know what, Arkie? I think Ian would've liked it here."

ELEVEN

No sooner was the hallway at home in Ramsay Street cluttered with the mess of suitcases, bags, clothes and blankets from the Batmobile, than someone was knocking at the front door.

"Wow, visitors already," mum marvelled, having settled herself at the kitchen table with a cup of tea.

"I'll get it," Arkie volunteered, and picked her way through the luggage to the front door. With windows open again, the house was beginning to lose its musty, closed atmosphere, and Goodvibes had wasted little time getting inside and seeking out one of his usual sleeping spots after a fortnight shut outdoors. "Stupid cat," Arkie muttered, nearly tripping over him in the hallway. As she went to open the front door, she heard Michael step in through the back door and say to mum, "Headley's not here —"

Arkie pulled the door open. Kylie and her mother stood out on the front step.

"Hi," Arkie said, and Mrs Bethel returned the greeting in a hesitant voice. Kylie flashed Arkie a quick glance and looked down.

"We have to see Michael," Kylie's mum said, almost nervously.

When Arkie's mum and Michael fronted up at the doorway, Mrs Bethel interrupted their well-meant hullos and spilled out a quick succession of events in an awkward and apologetic voice. It took a few moments to assimilate that Headley had disappeared and was still nowhere to be found.

"Kylie fed the pets for the first week," Mrs Bethel said, with Kylie nodding in agreement, "and took the dog out for a walk each day. But after last Thursday, there was no sign of him. She came up and found the chain and catch still here, but...it was as though someone had come and turned him loose."

"And I did the catch up properly," Kylie added emphatically. She would not look at anyone, especially Arkie, and seemed resentful of the whole situation.

"What about the pound?" Michael asked, suddenly looking as though two weeks of holidays hadn't happened at all.

"We've checked there twice. And there's an ad in this week's local paper."

Michael sighed and looked bewildered. "He should be around. He's just not energetic enough to wander off somewhere —"

"We're really sorry —" Mrs Bethel started to say, but Michael shook his head and dragged his wallet from the back pocket of his jeans.

"No, look, it was very kind of you to do all that. To go to all that trouble. Kylie, I owe you some money. Here's your thirty dollars."

Yeah Kylie, there's your thirty dollars.

"But —" Mrs Bethel faltered.

"No," Michael interrupted, "we agreed. You've done a great job, regardless of what happened. Headley'll turn up. Don't worry."

Arkie worried.

At the desk in her room, she laboriously printed three notices in multicoloured texta: *LOST, one male labrador bull terrier cross honey brown ten years old answers to name HEADLEY —*

Here she stopped, clutching the texta between her teeth. Standing at the window, she took in the fragmented view through the garden outside. The block of units next door were a completed shell now, windows installed with manufacturers' stickers plastered all over the glass. Glimpses of the interior showed unpainted cement walls and electrical wiring dangling from cavities; a wire fence had been installed in Arkie's absence, presumably to keep the neigbourhood kids at bay.

During the afternoon the sky had darkened, and now rain began to spatter against her window and drum on the carport roof. The light from the desk lamp spilled in a wide circle across her three LOST notices. In the loungeroom, mum had tinkled notes on the piano for a while, but now Arkie could hear only the steady voices of a documentary on television. Jo was pacing around the house restlessly, interested neither in TV or toys. Several times since their return, he had been down to Ian's place, bursting to tell holiday stories, but always returning and saying, "I knocked really loudly, but he wasn't there."

177

Arkie sighed heavily, and sat down at her desk once more.

Arkie and Jo dashed from the car to the covered walkway at the school's entrance, dodging puddles and expanses of mud to join the huddle of kids in yellow raincoats and soaked, inadequate sneakers. There were long lines for lunch orders in the canteen and a couple of teachers grumpily keeping everybody out of the rain.

How come it always feels like holidays have never happened once you get back to school?

"Hey, Arkie!" yelled out several voices in the echoed din of the canteen, and she found a group standing and sitting on wooden seats in one draughty corner.

"When did you get back?" asked Sally DeVries.

"Saturday arvo," Arkie replied, looking at Voula, Adam, Sean, Jodie Singleton breakfasting on a packet of crisps, and Eric.

"How was your holiday?"

"Great. Really good —"

"Jodie went away, didn't you Jode? And the rest of us hung around the skating rink or the park."

"We saw a couple of videos at Eric's place —"

"Saw a gory one at Sean's —"

"Hey, we heard about your dog —"

"Yeah, did he turn up?"

Arkie shook her head. "Not yet. We reckon maybe someone took him while we were away."

"Or Kylie let him loose deliberately," Adam Black suggested. "She'd do that, I reckon."

His opinion surprised Arkie, but she shook her head. Despite Kylie becoming so unpredictable lately, it was difficult to believe anything had been deliberate about Headley's disappearance.

"Yeah," Jodie Singleton went on, her mouth full of crisps, "and Kylie's been hanging out with this high school guy she and Rebecca met at the skating rink —"

"He looks about fifteen, but she reckons he's thirteen —"

"So she didn't hang around with us all through the holidays, she hung around with him."

"— turned into a bit of a snob, I reckon."

Arkie nodded in a resigned way, and looked out at the rain-drenched playground. On the other side, she could see her classroom.

"Hey and guess what," Eric said. "We've got a woman teacher."

"Huh? How d' you know?"

"I had to show her where the duplicating room was, didn't I?"

"Should see her, Arkie, she dresses like Mr Clifton —"

"She's a bit of a spunk," Adam said with a hopeful smirk. He was besieged with jeers.

"Hey Black, you got the hots for her or something?"

"Yeah, go and ask her to the movies, Adam —"

They trooped indoors at nine o'clock, and the new teacher leant against her desk and watched them sit down. Behind her on the blackboard was *Miss Tregear* in simple handwriting, as if she were issuing a reminder to a group of infants children. She spoke to them calmly and deliberately, but her eyes constantly flickered about the room, as if seeking out undercurrents of resentment or potential misbehaviour.

Some of the kids were helpful.

"There's a bucket in the storeroom," Sally DeVries advised when Miss Tregear commented about the leaky roof and the dampening corner of carpet. "Mr Clifton always had the bucket set up under the leak whenever it rained."

"Can we change seats?" Rebecca asked. "Mr Clifton said we could after the holidays." She and Kylie exchanged glances.

The whole class had their eyes trained on the new teacher. "Not quite yet," Miss Tregear answered steadily. "I'd like to get to know you all first." She was slight and pencil-thin, had more earrings than Mr Clifton and a clever combination of clothes that had a slight air of St Vincent de Paul about them.

She read the list of names from the roll. When she got to Ian Koh's name, she looked over at the only vacant chair in the whole room and asked, "Does anyone know where he is? Is he still away on holidays?"

From somewhere there came a slight snigger, and someone replied, "We haven't seen him, Miss."

"You'll like Ian when he arrives, but," Sean Taylor announced in a false tone of voice. "He likes helping teachers."

"Yeah," Adam continued cynically, "he's a real big help around the classroom, miss."

She looked at them with a slight frown and

said, "That's enough, I think," before continuing her way down the list of names.

With rain continuing to rattle on the classroom roof, they settled down to written work and stencils. Miss Tregear thumbed through some of their exercise books, and when she made occasional comments, perfect silence fell over the room as if people were still judging and making up their minds about her.

Kylie had not said much at all since arriving at school, and now was hunched over a stencil, her hands under her chin.

Arkie turned and asked quietly, "What's up?"

Kylie shrugged and replied, "Nothing. I wish Mr Clifton was still here."

Arkie grimaced. "How was your holiday?"

"Alright," Kylie said in a distinterested voice, and would say no more.

Arkie looked back at her own stencil, but her mind was tumbling with thoughts beyond schoolwork. She was bursting to tell someone about her holidays, but there was no-one around who'd listen and appreciate all that had happened. She stole another quiet look at Kylie. *I wish I was back on the verandah at John and Carol's. Warming up next to the wood stove. Feeding the sheep. There were paddocks where a whole town had been. Five kids living in a doubledecker bus with their mum. A little cave full of a dead man's things. Mum's going to play in a band. We came home and found our dog missing.*

She pinned one of her LOST notices up on the message board in the school library. On the way home from school that afternoon, she asked the newsagent to tape another notice up in the front window, and then walked on with Jo to the milkbar, where she gave the last of the notices to Robert Checcutti's mum to stickytape to the window next to the cigarette and icecream posters.

"I'm gonna play the machines," Jo announced when Arkie began to walk on.

She frowned in annoyance and said, "Hurry up then, will you?"

The traffic splashed by on the road, stopping for the lights at the intersection and then rumbling and groaning away once more. Everything within sight and feeling was wet, cold and grey. Leaving Jo to punch and prod at a space invaders machine, she walked on a short distance. Passing the windows of the laundromat, she vaguely registered the rows of washing machines and tumble dryers and then saw, on one of the plastic chairs next to the table with piles of crumpled magazines, someone who hadn't been at school that day.

"Hey Ian," she said, stepping into the warmth, the soapy fragrance and the hum of machines, "Why weren't you at school today? Holiday's finished, you know."

Ian had been reading a magazine, and looked up with surprise and mild alarm. "I was — I got a cold," he answered quickly.

"Doesn't sound like it," Arkie replied, and sat down next to him.

He edged away slightly. "Well, I have."

"Are you gonna be at school tomorrow?"

182

"I dunno."

"Why are you here?"

"I had to bring the washing down. Mum said to."

"Where is she?"

"Gone...visiting. She said she'd be back in a few days."

"You can come up to our place if you like. Jo's been looking for you."

She expected an enthusiastic reply to this, but Ian looked down at his magazine and replied, "No, it's okay."

He wouldn't look up again, so Arkie leant right over and craned her face up at his. "Hey, what's wrong? You're acting funny."

"Nothing," he said, annoyed but in a soft voice. "You're asking too many questions. Leave me alone."

Arkie sighed and sat back up. Clothes swirled around in the portholes of the spin dryers. The proprietor sat over at her counter, puffing distractedly at a cigarette and taking in some afternoon TV. Two other people sat waiting for their washing, smoking and gazing at the television in the same bored silence.

"Jo's next door in Checcutti's playing the machines," Arkie said then, standing up and hitching her schoolbag over one shoulder, "and it's cold and wet outside. I have to get home; see you." At the doorway, she paused and added, "By the way, Headley's gone missing and there's a reward if you find him."

She walked out quickly, without waiting for a

reaction or reply. When she passed by the laundromat window a second time, Jo behind her, Ian had gone.

Headley did not turn up that day or the next, and an uncharacteristic gloom cracked Michael's usual calm facade.

"We looked on the way home," Jo said during the evening meal. "Arkie and me walked a different way home and we looked."

Michael nodded.

"But Headley'd know the way home," Jo continued, "and he wouldn't have gone away with just anyone."

"Jo," mum said, "we've been through this already."

"Did you phone the dog pound?" Jo persisted. "Maybe someone —"

"Jo," mum said emphatically, "give it a rest, mate."

Jo pulled an only-trying-to-be-helpful face. "Well..."

Michael leant his elbows on the table and said, "All we can do is keep looking, waiting and hoping, I guess."

"None of our pets has ever gone missing before," Jo mumbled down at the tablecloth.

"He's Michael's dog, really. We never had any pets before Goodvibes and Headley, anyway," Arkie reminded him, and at that, Michael scraped his chair back from the table and stood up.

"You okay?" mum asked.

Michael raised his eyebrows. "Yeah, I'm alright. D' you mind if I move the Citroen out of

184

the driveway? I might start the ute up and go for a drive around the neighbourhood. Headley might be hanging out somewhere with his doggy mates or something." He managed a slight smile and went outside.

Presently, they heard the Batmobile being reversed out from under the carport. Minutes later, there came a rhythmic whine and then a choking rumble, as the old Holden came to life.

"He hasn't driven that thing for ages," mum said, as its sound faded away down the street.

Mrs Bethel's advertisements in the local paper brought no phone calls, and no-one at school dashed up to Arkie or Jo to report sighting Headley.

At home, when mum gave Arkie the vacuuming to do, it seemed that nothing but honey-coloured dog hair caught itself on the vacuum brush.

TWELVE

Headley, the day I got him, one of a litter of five equally dopey looking pups.

Headley's favourite occupation (age four months) — chewing record covers.

Our household, third semester of uni —Karen (social science), Lenny (arts), Margaret (arts), me (teaching, ha ha), Headley the dog (gluttony).

"So that's who lived here before us," Arkie whispered to herself, looking at Michael's handwriting on the back of each snapshot. She had fished out another envelope of photographs from a drawer in the roll-top desk, and paused to examine the photo of the previous household. There were three people she didn't know and a younger Michael, whose hair was blonder and whose bald patch was not quite so noticeable. Arkie smiled.

"Do you want a game of Scrabble?" mum had asked her that Wednesday afternoon when they had all returned home from school. Jo had been nagging her for a game.

"I've got homework," Arkie replied and had quietly closed her bedroom door, turning her

186

attention to the desk and its contents. She could hear mum and Jo setting their game up out on the dining table. Michael had wandered down to the service station.

She slipped the photos back into their envelope and pulled another package from the desk drawer.

Graduation Ball, the first time I ever wore a bow tie (and probably the last!).

Ian Koh, Ramsay Street waif and unofficial household member. We feed him now and again; he once spent the night on the loungeroom couch when his mother didn't return home.

Ian, younger than Jo. Ian with pudgy cheeks and a grubby face.

Ian K. (four) with Headley (two).

Ian with Headley in the backyard, when it had been more a tangle of grass, without a garden of any description. Ian grinning broadly, Headley with an entirely normal dopey dog expression.

There was a folded up painting in the envelope too, a small child's tangle of exuberant colour and smiling face. *I like playing with Headley the dog*, it said in neat teacher's script at the base of the picture. *To Michael*, it said on the back, in partially reversed child's handwriting.

There were voices outside. Michael had returned with Evan, one of the garage mechanics. Together they pored over the engine compartment of the Batmobile and then of Michael's utility. Arkie heard their footsteps, saw them passing by the veil of shrubs before her window. She put the painting and photos back in their package and into the drawer. Michael and Evan walked inside, discussing cars and model faults, and settled themselves in the kitchen, Evan having obviously finished work for the day.

I don't feel like homework yet. Maybe Scrabble would be alright. Arkie opened her bedroom door again, but hesitated in the hallway when she heard Evan the mechanic say, "A weird thing, you know —" He clicked open a can of beer Michael had handed him. "Cheers, mate. A weird thing —"

"Like what?" Michael asked.

"Like a guy I had in after petrol this morning. He lives in the Seaview units and was saying someone there's had a dog shut up in one of the flats for days now."

"Eh?"

"A dog. They can hear it scuttling around, whining and barking. Who'd be loopy enough to keep a dog in that place? There'd be trouble if the real estate people got to hear about it."

Ian K. (four) with Headley (two). Arkie looked out the front door, down the length of Ramsay Street, at the Seaview units wedged down near the main road, and an answer to Headley's whereabouts suddenly teased at her.

Michael was leaning against the kitchen sink, taking a measured sip from a can of beer. "Has anyone seen the dog?" he asked Evan, "because my dog's been missing for about a week now."

Evan shook his head. He had a service station uniform on and grease under his fingernails. "No-one. The guy I was talking to seemed to think some kid had it, but."

"Ian," Arkie said from the doorway.

Michael looked at her.

"Ian," she repeated, and Michael's eyes widened. He nodded. "He hasn't been at school all week —" she added.

"— and he hasn't been up here to visit all week," Michael finished. He put his beer can down, went into the loungeroom and returned with a book, which he handed to Evan. "Here's the one about the history of Citroens, did you still want t' borrow it?"

"Yeah," Evan answered, speaking into his beer can.

"I've got to go out for a minute. I'll catch up with you later," Michael added. To Arkie, he said, "D' you want to come for a walk?"

They left the house and walked quickly downhill, footsteps clicking almost in time on the footpath. The peak-hour traffic on the main road had started to filter back from the city, and a sea breeze pushed up from the coastline. Even from a distance, the rust and rain stains stood out prominently on the Seaview's white brickwork. At its entrance, a group of little kids were playing with a pocket computer game, and Michael and Arkie stopped to listen for any telltale dog noises from inside the building. Nothing.

"You kids seen a dog around here?" Michael asked, but the children gaped at him blankly and shook their heads. To Arkie, he said in a low voice, "What made you think of Ian?"

"He hasn't been back to school and no-one's

seen him, except me just once. He was in the laundromat on Monday, but he was acting funny and wouldn't say anything."

They began to climb the stairs. "What if his mum's home?" Arkie said. "What if Ian doesn't have Headley after all?" Michael raised his eyebrows thoughtfully. "Don't worry, I'll do the talking."

The crimson staircase carpet smelt of salt air and mildew. There were initials and scribble on the stairwell walls and handprints around the doorhandle to Ian's flat.

A television was on inside, but Michael's knock on the door at first brought no response. He knocked again, and a door within clicked shut. Then the front door opened and Ian peered out.

"Hullo," he said in a small voice, looking totally stricken at the sight of Arkie and Michael.

"Thought you might still be sick," Arkie started. "Haven't seen you all week and . . ."

Ian said nothing.

Michael sighed. "We also wanted to ask you if you'd seen Headley. He's still not turned up and we heard — someone said that there was a dog here somewhere whining and barking."

Ian was already shaking his head. "All I ever hear is people —"

His mum's not here, Arkie thought to herself, but she couldn't be sure, because Ian had the door open only a short distance. And then abruptly, there was a scratching noise from somewhere down the hallway, frantic animal scratching. The stricken look on Ian's face intensified and he

190

grasped the door, beginning to close it. The scrambling, scratching continued and then there was a bark, shrill and piercing.

Michael spoke carefully, reluctantly. "Ian, is that Headley in there?"

Ian stared at the floor, shuddered and burst into tears. Michael said nothing more for a moment, and he looked down also.

"Arkie," he said quietly, "could you go in and let Headley out for me?"

Cautiously, Arkie eased past Ian. The lounge-room curtains were closed, and she peered around the corner at the flickering TV screen, crumpled up chip packets and soft drink cans on the floor. Ian's mum's bedroom lay opposite, darkened and empty. She turned around to the closed door that shut Ian's bedroom off, noticing a vague odour of wet dog. *Like Headley after he's been out in the rain.* When the bedroom door was opened, Headley sprang out into the hallway, whimpering, grovelling and tail-wagging around Arkie's feet. Then he bounded up to Michael and repeated the glad-to-see-you performance, adding leaps in the air as a bonus. Ian was still hunched over crying at the doorway.

"Ian," Michael said, "is your mum around?"

Ian shook his head, crying in heaving sobs and sniffles. He was clutching the door so tightly that the knuckles on his hand were white, and Arkie shifted about uncomfortably, unable to look at him for too long. *I don't like people crying, I'm not used to it.*

After a pause, and in a gasping voice, Ian replied, "I don't know. She said she'd be back last Saturday. She left me money —"

"You can't stay here by yourself any more," Michael said in a tight voice. "Come home with us, mate. Go and grab some of your things."

Ian didn't answer or move. He'd almost stopped crying; the front of his jacket was covered in spatters of tear stains.

Michael knelt down. "Ian," he said softly, "come here." The two of them locked together in a hug, Ian's face buried in Michael's jumper, Michael's chin resting on Ian's shoulder. When they released each other, Ian walked up the hallway to his bedroom. Michael stood up. "It's sad," he said to Arkie, "just sad." To Headley, he added, "Will you stop leaping at me, you bloody twit?" But he rubbed a gentle hand over the dog's head.

Evan the mechanic awkwardly excused himself and left when the strange entourage arrived back at the house.

"Hey, Ian!" Jo said loudly, abandoning his game of scrabble, "I've been looking for you all —" but he fell silent as Michael motioned with one hand.

"How about looking after Ian for a while?" Michael suggested. "Take him upstairs to your room or something."

Headley wriggled free of the grasp Arkie had around his collar. He bounded noisily through the front door and began trotting in and out of each downstairs room.

192

"Hey, where was...?" Jo shrieked excitedly, but Michael motioned again for quiet. Puzzled, Jo walked over and said in an uncertain voice, "Come on, Ian." Ian followed without a word and the two of them climbed the stairs.

Mum's concerned expression flickered from Ian to Michael, as if she had immediately understood the course of events. She went over and turned the radio on, mumbling, "This place needs brightening up." Then to Michael, she said in a low voice, "So that's where the dog's been?"

Headley trotted back into the loungeroom, and sat himself down on the floor, tail thrashing. Michael knelt down and scratched at the fur behind Headley's ears. "Yes," he answered wearily.

Mum was shaking her head. "So what are you thinking, Mike?"

"I don't know what to think."

"Where's his mother?"

"Not there."

"What about the pub?"

"I didn't look. Ian said she'd gone, telling him she'd be back Saturday."

Mum sat down on the floor next to Michael. Arkie settled in the nearest armchair and asked, "D' you want me to go down and see if she's at the pub?"

"No, stay here," mum replied, and added in a hushed, annoyed voice, "What's happened this year? That child has spent most of the last twelve months on his own."

Michael shook his head.

"We can't," mum continued, "we can't go on covering for his mother. How long has she been gone this time?"

"Over a week," Michael answered. "She left him this." And he pulled from his pocket two ten dollar notes folded into small squares.

Mum looked away. "Mike, it's getting out of hand. The child eats and sleeps here. What happens at school, Arkie?"

Startled out of listening, Arkie replied hesitantly, "The kids tease him and leave him out of everything. They nick his schoolbag and hide it —"

"We have to tell someone," mum said, keeping her voice low so that it wouldn't carry upstairs. "We've been the ones taking care of him for months and months. Where's the school been?"

"They've been without a counsellor for ages," Michael reminded her. "Government cutbacks, remember."

"Well, I'm mentioning it to Glenda when she comes in to school next Monday, then. Even though she's working her fingers to the bone and there's a line of high school kids a mile long she's seeing and trying to sort out already..." Her voice became more subdued. "I've got yoga this evening. What's happening with Ian tonight?"

"He's staying," Michael said with a shrug. "I'll sort out a bed for him in Jo's room. He can't stay any longer in that flat by himself."

Mum sighed. "And he had Headley cooped up in there all this time?"

"I don't know," Michael said, shaking his head, "I'll talk to him later."

194

When Arkie went upstairs to use the bathroom, she peered around the doorway to Jo's room. Jo was aimlessly pushing toy cars around on the mat, while Ian sat nearby, trancelike and silent.

She went back to her own room then, and pulled the holiday suitcase down from on top of her wardrobe. From one of the inside pockets she brought out the photograph found in the rock crevice. The child with the black hair and dark eyes stared and smiled back at her. Quickly, she read the writing on the back again. Now that she looked more closely, there were lots of little fingerprints on the photo's white card backing. It had been held and looked at many times. She clunked the suitcase back up onto the wardrobe, but carefully and reverently placed the photo in the Atrocity Cabinet, between the souvenir snowstorms and the amputee Barbie doll.

She sat on the couch beneath her bedroom window, and tried to concentrate on reading a book from the school library. "What d' you want?" she had to ask wearily, because Jo was suddenly hanging around the doorway.

"I just came down to look at your room," he said in a sombre voice. "Michael's upstairs talking to Ian."

"Oh."

"Arkie —"

"Yeah?"

"— are you telling any of the kids at school about Ian taking Headley?"

"Of course not. Are you?"

"No. . ."

"Good. And if you're gonna hang around in my room, don't mess around with my things."

Offended, Jo wrinkled his nose at her. After a pause though, he added, "It's nice in here."

Later, in the kitchen, as mum pulled a sweater on over her leotard, she said, "What a strange day this has been."

Michael rested himself against the fridge. "You're telling me."

Outside came the rattle of chain, as Headley gave up on being let back inside and wandered over the paving stone to his kennel.

"Any homework tonight, Arkie?" mum asked.

"You bet," Arkie replied. On purpose, she was taking ages to finish wiping the dishes on the sink.

"How's the new teacher?"

"Okay, I guess. Sometimes she's like those student teachers we get, but."

Mum shrugged. "You lot might be her very first class, then. Lucky woman, she is." Mum glanced at her watch. "Look, I have to go, I'll be late."

"Yeah, see you."

"Bye, mum."

"See you guys later," came mum's voice in the loungeroom. Jo and Ian were both in pyjamas by now, and engrossed in a TV programme. The front door clicked shut and there was the sound of the Batmobile starting up, manoeuvring out of the driveway and setting off down the street.

Arkie finished wiping up, and went to her room to dig out her homework.

"It'd be quieter in your room," Michael suggested when he saw her setting her things down on the dining table.

"I want t' be out here," she replied, watching as Michael strolled over to the couch and sat down next to Ian. Ian flinched and edged away slightly, looking at Michael warily.

Did Michael get cranky with him?

Jo stood up and stepped over the couch cushions, sitting himself on Michael's other side. Ian edged himself back next to Michael.

Huh, the usual stuff. Both of them after his attention. Ian looked odd in pyjamas, more like a little child than the twelve-year-old he was.

And I bet Adam Black looks weird in pyjamas, too.

For a while, there were only the voices from the television, advertisements and background music. In between scribbling halfhearted answers across a stencil, Arkie glanced at the calm scene beside her — Michael, Jo and Ian settled on the couch and staring at the TV screen.

Eventually, Michael said, "Bedtime, you two," to Jo and Ian, and gently shooed them upstairs. "I'll be up there shortly."

There were footsteps on the staircase, and then taps and things being turned on and off. Michael followed them up to say goodnight and turn lights out. When he came downstairs once more, it was slowly and thoughtfully.

"Is he all right?" Arkie asked.

Michael stared at the television for a moment more, switched it off, and dug a record out of the shelf under the stereo. "Who, Ian? He's okay. Washed out and very tired, though." Michael flicked a couple of switches on, placed the record on the turntable and wound the volume down, so that the music trickled quietly into the room. He sat at the table next to Arkie, and said, "He'd been taking Headley out for walks late at night — around the shopping centre, along the beach." He paused and shook his head slowly.

"Were you angry at him?"

"No, I wasn't angry at him."

"Did he take Headley, though?"

Michael nodded. "He came up here one evening and took him for a walk and just...didn't come back. When I asked him about it earlier, that's all he could put into words. It's such a strange thing for him to have done, but I can understand why."

"Why?"

Michael looked at her and said plainly, "He's scared of being by himself."

Arkie chewed at the end of her pen. "What's going to happen?"

"I don't know." He paused again. "Welfare were involved with him and his mum once before. When Ian was about four, he was put into foster care for a while, so that his mum could sort herself and her drinking out. She just wasn't coping —"

"What about Ian's dad?"

"Ian's mum doesn't know who Ian's dad is. A few guys have moved into their flat over the years,

198

and Ian's got to call each of them dad, but they've always wound up moving out."

Arkie hesitated. "That's what I used t' think it'd be like with you." *Why did I say that?*

"With me?" Michael said in a surprised voice. "How?"

Arkie shrugged. "When I was nine or something, I wondered —" *Don't say any more.* "— I thought that you'd leave, too."

"Do you still think that?"

"No, 'course not. But it happened to other kids at school. It happened to Kylie." *It happened to us.*

Michael looked at her, worried and thoughtful. "This is my home, Arkie. And you're the family I'm part of."

They fell silent.

My dad left and I remember it happening. She aimlessly coloured at the lettering on her homework stencil. "What's going to happen with Ian, though?"

"I don't know. It makes me so angry... not with Ian himself. With the situation. There are so many kids like Ian around. Your mum and I see them at school every day of the week, and no matter how much you do to try and help them, it always boils down to them being other people's children." His eyes flickered over at hers. "Thanks for looking after Ian all this time, Arkie."

Arkie frowned. "I don't look after him. Jo has more to do with him than me." *Once, I said to Kylie, 'Ian? He's alright.'*

"I think you have," Michael told her, "in ways you don't realise."

Arkie started to gather her stencils and pens together. *Ian's mum doesn't know who Ian's dad is.*

"Off to bed?"

"Yeah," she replied, sighing.

"Half your luck. I've got year eleven essays to set by tomorrow. Urk."

Arkie stood up and Michael stood up also, hugging her briefly and kissing her lightly on the forehead.

From her bedroom, she heard him walk out to the kitchen, and make himself a cup of coffee.

THIRTEEN

It was Monday before she remembered to take her LOST notice down from the message board in the school library.

"Where was your dog, anyway?" Voula asked.

"Dunno," Arkie replied, deciding to fabricate the answer. "Ian found him."

"Was your dog the one people in the Seaview units were complaining about?"

"Who knows? I don't think so."

Ian's return to school coincided more or less with his mother's return from points unknown. Adam Black, who had been organising water fights in the boys' toilets before school, and was yet to be sprung by the teachers, yelled, "Hey Crawler Koh, how come you aren't waiting in the carpark before school any more?"

Ian went into the canteen and joined the lines of kids waiting to order their lunches. Adam and a couple of other kids followed him.

"Hey," Adam continued loudly, "and why aren't you in the classroom doing jobs for the new teacher? When are you gonna start crawling to her like you did to Mr Clifton?"

Ian didn't answer.

"Hey, Koh —"

"Yeah, you with the girlie hair —"

"Aren't you talking to us any more?"

Miss Tregear looked pleased about finally meeting her elusive student. At first when she spoke to him in class or asked him something, his replies were a hushed mumble, and she tried pressing him to speak more slowly and clearly. Her requests didn't help.

He hardly ever looks at her. Arkie realised it suddenly one morning when she sat watching him. *He hardly ever looks at anybody, really.*

Miss Tregear finally relented on the seating arrangements, and so the din began, with kids emptying their desks out and yelling to one another across the room.

"You're supposed to be doing this quietly and sensibly!" she said loudly, looking as though she regretted the whole idea.

Kylie emptied her desk and moved over next to Rebecca within a matter of seconds; they sat looking smugly at each other and Arkie tried not to glance in their direction. She had begun to gather her own possessions with the intention of sitting next to Voula, but stopped with dismay, seeing that Voula already had someone else sitting next to her.

This is bad news. Arkie sighed. She noted that a whole group of boys had arranged themselves into a corner area of desks. *Miss Tregear, you could regret this.*

Gradually, the room began to settle. As if fulfilling some prearranged dares, a few girls had found themselves boys to sit next to, and were flashing conspiring grins around the classroom. The floor was covered in paper, stencils and pens dropped, and a few kids were still wandering around trying to find themselves new seats.

"You have," Miss Tregear was saying in an edgy voice, "one minute to organise yourselves."

I give up, Arkie thought gloomily, remaining in her original seat, with the adjoining place still vacant. Self-consciously she glanced about at the rest of the class and saw that Ian also remained, by himself, at his own desk. At that moment, Sally DeVries and another girl were staring about and whingeing, "But Miss, there's no desks we can sit at."

Arkie did some quick thinking.

This is it for the rest of the year. I'm going to get stirred. Adam and Sean and the others'll start writing stuff on toilet walls and bus stop seats. I'm going to get laughed at.

Hastily, she gathered her books and pencil case, stood up and walked over to the vacant seat at Ian's desk.

"Hey, check Arkie out!"

"Woooo, Arkie!"

She sat down grimacing, and Ian stared at her with suspicion all over his face, as if a prank of some sort was being played out.

"Why are you sitting here?" he whispered, staring at the desk top.

"Because I want to," she answered flippantly, almost sure it was the truth. Around her, the cheers and derogatory remarks became a deafening roar.

"That's quite enough!" Miss Tregear shouted, slamming the classroom door for effect. "This is sixth class, not preschool!"

The noise dropped to a few discreet giggles.

"We're very sorry, miss," Sean Taylor called out with mock sincerity.

"If you want to be clever, Mr Taylor, maybe a few lunchtime detentions will sort you out," Miss Tregear added severely.

"Oh no miss, I'll behave," answered Sean in his same tone of voice, and sat up with exaggerated straightness, so that there were continued giggles from the rest of the kids.

Miss Tregear managed to get a lesson underway.

"Two more months in this dump," someone behind Arkie whispered.

Another voice whispered, "Yeah, roll on high school."

Arkie tried coaxing conversation out of Ian, but he seemed either shy or annoyed about her sitting next to him.

He wears that same tracksuit almost every day. His hair's got little streaks of orange through it when you look closely, and he pushes it behind his ear when he's leaning over doing schoolwork. Sometimes he copies my answers when we're doing maths.

"Can I borrow your textas?" she asked one afternoon.

"Yeah, sure," Ian replied softly, and reached

for them under his desk. Tattooed all over the vinyl pencilcase's exterior was the same abstract pattern Arkie had seen on the card he had made for Mr Clifton.

At lunchtimes, without fail, he'd meet up with Jo in the school library, whilst the remainder of the class took their restlessness to the back playground for wild games of chasings and volleyball.

"There's stuff about you and Ian written on the seat at the bus stop," Kylie remarked casually to Arkie on the way home one day.

Arkie glanced about, but the other kids seemed to be involved in their own conversations. The novelty of the new seating arrangements at school had worn off slightly. "Big deal," she replied.

Ian and Jo stopped off at the takeaway for a round on the machines, and Arkie took herself to the newsagent's. She bought a thick black texta and a large sheet of bright yellow project cardboard. Stepping outside, she walked up to where the bus stop seat was. Sean Taylor's message of several months before had been completed so that it now read *Arkie G. loves Ian K. true.* Uncapping her new texta, she scribbled the message out. She wanted to write "*Sean T. loves himself*" instead, but a woman with a handful of shopping walked up and sat down on the seat.

They straggled up Ramsay Street.

"What's the cardboard for?" Jo asked.

"It's for Ian," Arkie replied. She turned to him. "I wanted to know if you could make me a card."

"What for?"

"It's our mum's birthday next Saturday," Arkie explained, "and I wanted you to make a card like...that other one you made. The one with the pattern."

"Oh, that," he said, looking down.

"Well?" she asked. "Can you make me one? You're better at art than me."

He shrugged. "I guess so."

They let themselves into the house and went upstairs to Jo's room. Arkie measured and cut a rectangle out of the cardboard sheet, carefully folded the rectangle in half and gave it to Ian. He dug around in his school bag for his textas and then spread himself out on the floor. Arkie went downstairs and returned with her camera.

"What've you got that for?" Ian grumbled.

"To take a picture, stupid," she replied, settling on the floor opposite. "It's the last picture on the film." A texta pattern had begun to consume the yellow cardboard and beside Ian, Jo worked as well, drawing a picture of spacecraft and rocket fire in an old schoolbook.

"Mum's having a party on Saturday night," Arkie told him, setting the camera's dials.

"I know," he replied, not taking his eyes from what he was drawing. "Jo told me."

"I'm starving myself all day Saturday," Jo announced, "so I can eat lots of party food. Are you still gonna come, Ian?"

"Maybe."

Arkie lay on the floor and arched the camera at Ian's preoccupied face. Jo was slightly blurred and in the background; the moment both boys looked expectantly at her, she pressed the shutter button.

"Great," she mumbled, and began to wind the film off.

There was the slightest hint of a smile on Ian's face as he renewed concentration on his drawing.

Mr Clifton always made a fuss over Ian's artwork. And maybe Michael used to make a fuss too; that folded-up painting I found in one of the photo envelopes...

Mum put the birthday card up on top of the piano on Saturday morning after she had opened her presents. It was still there, in clear view, when dusk came and the loungeroom began to fill with people.

Some guests arrived that Arkie didn't recognise. They came through the front door hesitantly, a group of five or six guys and girls in their late teens, who stood looking about selfconsciously. One of them said loudly, "Hey, there's the birthday girl. Happy birthday, Mrs Gerhardt!"

A lot of the adults turned to the group and directed caustic remarks across the room.

"Agh, we're being invaded by year twelve —"

"Who invited you lot?"

"There's an age limit here, y' know —"

But Arkie's mum wandered over and said, "What's this Mrs Gerhardt stuff? Your final exams start in a matter of weeks and then you're finished with school forever. My name's Susan —"

Some of mum's music pupils, the ones whose stuff mum brings home to mark. The ones she says nice things about. Other people's children, Michael said.

Jo was making sporadic trips downstairs to raid the food set out on the table, and then racing back upstairs again because he was watching something on the portable TV in mum's and Michael's room. The adults stood in groups around the loungeroom talking, and there was already a haze of tobacco smoke hanging overhead. The noise was gradually escalating, someone had turned up the volume on the stereo. Even when she walked out into the kitchen, Arkie could hear Michael locked in uproarious conversation and mum somewhere nearby, laughing.

She smiles and laughs a fair bit. Not like Kylie's mum, who always looks tired or grumpy about something. And Ian's mum, whose voice I haven't ever heard.

"Did you ask Kylie along?" her mum asked, stepping into the kitchen. Her eyes were sparkly and relaxed.

Arkie shook her head.

"Why not?" mum asked.

"I just didn't."

Her mum looked at her strangely for a moment, before saying, "I meant to say to you before that a mystery guest'll be along tonight."

"Who?"

"Someone Michael met up with while he was out shopping this week."

"Is it someone I know?"

"Sure is."

"Well, who?"

"It wouldn't be a mystery if I told you. And come out and talk to a few people; hanging around in kitchens isn't a habit I want you to cultivate."

Mum's ex-pupils were by now more confident in their adult surroundings, and getting noisy. *It's funny how parties make some people really loud and others get really quiet and sit by themselves.*

Arkie kept an eye on the front door. *Who's the mystery guest, then?* One of mum's and Michael's fellow teachers came up to her and said, "I've been hearing about your photography."

Arkie looked at her blankly for moment, a woman in carnival-bright clothes, and not much taller than Arkie was. "I've been taking a few photos," she answered awkwardly. *What a stupid reply.*

"What, colour or black and white?"

"Black and white." *And blurry, probably.*

"And what sort of things d' you take pictures of?"

Arkie shrugged. "Just people. My family. The kids in our street." *And other things I've seen that no-one else has.*

"And you'll be at our high school next year, won't you? If you're still interested by then, I've been running a photography group at lunchtimes. We've got a darkroom set up, so it's not just taking photos but developing them as well. How have your pictures been turning out?"

"I dunno. I've only just finished my first roll."

"Well, you'll be very welcome to join the group. I've heard a lot about you from Susan —"

What's mum been saying now? But Arkie's attention was diverted by the sight of someone through the windows over near the front door. The person hesitated at the doorway and looked around the room. His clothes veered close to masquerade.

"Mr Clifton!" Arkie called, and he smiled back at her.

He had a black dinner suit on, a white shirt, black bow tie and sandshoes. In one hand was a bunch of flowers, which he presented to Arkie's mum when she went over to greet him.

He looks different.

"How come you're all dressed up?" she asked him shyly when he walked over.

He was already armed with a glass of wine and a handful of crisps. "I just like dressing up sometimes."

"I thought you were going travelling or something."

He shook his head. "Not yet. I've been taking it easy for a few weeks, but I'm setting off up north at the end of the month. So, what's been happening, Arkie? How's school?"

"Alright. The new teacher's okay, but the kids are playing up on her a bit." She looked at Mr Clifton, surveying his face and hair. "What happened to your hair? It's kind of . . . shaggy. Like you stuck your fingers in a power point or something." She giggled at her own humour.

Mr Clifton pulled a face. "Thanks!" He fell silent then, and looked around. "I like your house. Very much. You used to tell me about it —"

"It's almost the only house in the street. Every thing else is home units, and we used t' have a vacant block right next door, but now there's home units on that, too." She paused. Someone turned the stereo up louder still. "What's it like where you live?"

"An inner city terrace. There's five of us sharing it, and the rent is a total rip-off. The rooms leak air and rain and we have a problem with cockroaches." He grinned crookedly. "I should catch you some for your Atrocity Cabinet."

"Yuk, Mr Clifton."

"Can I see this famous Atrocity Cabinet? You brought a few things from it into school once for those Friday talks —"

"My room's a bit messy," she cautioned.

"I don't mind. Compared to my house, anything's tidy."

She went and turned her bedroom light on, hastily kicking a pair of sandshoes and dirty socks under her bed. Mr Clifton knelt down by the Atrocity Cabinet, slid the glass door open and looked at each of the exhibits. He laughed about the collection of souvenir snowstorms. "One of the people at my place collects stuff like this — snowstorms, 3-D postcards, garden gnomes..." His eyes moved to the black and white baby photo, and he picked it out of the cabinet, reading the inscription on the back.

Arkie took an audible breath.

"Who's this?" Mr Clifton asked. "Not your dad?"

"No," she replied, framing words quickly, "I found it during the August holidays."

"Found it? Where?"

She met his gaze uncomfortably. "In a cave. There was whole lot of stuff there, and it all belonged to some kids whose father...no-one else knows about it —"

"I can keep secrets," he said.

So haltingly, she talked about the farmhouse, the remains of a town, the plains, paddocks and endless hills, Jean Arcana and her five children, their bus and the rock crevice with its gallery of objects.

He shook his head slowly. "That's amazing," he said, placing the photo back in the cabinet. "Are you keeping this?"

"It doesn't belong here," Arkie said. "I'm taking it back when we go up there next. At Christmas maybe, mum said."

Out in the hallway, Mr Clifton asked, "How's Ian?"

"Same as usual. I think he misses you." *The whole class does.*

"I think you understand him better than the others," Mr Clifton told her, oddly self-conscious. "That's why I asked."

"He was supposed to be there tonight. We asked him —" Then she added quickly, as inspiration struck, "I'll go and get him, he lives just down the road."

She strode through the people and noise in the loungeroom and out the front door. The party seemed to follow her down the hill, music, talk and laughter rising above the snatches of TV emanating from home unit windows she passed. There was a vague taste of traffic fumes in the air, and the unpleasant smell of garbage in the plastic bins

212

beside buildings. The entrance lights and a lone stairwell lamp were on when she reached the Seaview units, and she clambered up the garishly carpeted stairs. Light glimmered from underneath the door to Ian's unit and she could hear the TV from somewhere within — soap opera voices in hackneyed dispute.

I hope his mum's not here. She began to knock on the door, but found it unexpectedly unlocked and open. "Ian?" she said, pushing it ajar and knowing her voice had been too soft for anyone to have heard. "Are you here?"

The main room's light was on and quickly, her eyes found the unfolded washing on the kitchen table, Ian's schoolbag flung on the couch, the fliptop kitchen tidy overflowing with empty cans and packets and the TV table minus the TV. Light flickered from the nearest bedroom doorway and within, Ian sat sprawled on his bed with a blanket drawn up around his chin. The TV was on a chair at the foot of the bed. He had obviously heard someone else in the flat, because his expectant gaze met Arkie's inquisitive one.

"What're you doing in bed, Ian? It's early."

"There was something on TV. What did you want?"

There were motorcycle posters and Ian's artwork stickytaped awkwardly to the wall next to his bed. A wardrobe lay open, overflowing with crumpled clothes.

"I just...my mum's party's on and you said you were going to be there."

Ian shrugged.

"Are you coming up?"

213

He hesitated and then said slowly, "No, I'll stay here."

"Ian, just for a while."

"Why?"

"There's someone up there I reckon you'd like to see."

"Who?"

"I'm not saying. Just...come on. I'm not waiting all night."

Ian gave her an almost grumpy look, before kicking the blanket off, leaning forward and flicking the TV switch and springing off the bed. She had half-expected to see him in pyjamas, but he had a T-shirt and jeans on.

"Where's your mum?" she asked.

"Down at the pub," he answered with a sigh, disconnecting the TV and carrying it back into the loungeroom.

The blind was drawn over the bedroom window and idly Arkie went over and jerked at it so that it sprang up wildly. The view outside was of the flats next door.

They walked up Ramsay Street and entered the noisy loungeroom. Mr Clifton was on the other side of the room talking with a couple of people.

"See the guy over there in the penguin suit?" Arkie said, but Ian had already spotted Mr Clifton. "Well, go on," She said as he hesitated. "Go over and talk to him."

Ian stood perfectly still for a moment longer, and then slowly began threading his way between the groups of people.

"Heeeyyy!" Mr Clifton said loudly, as Ian walked silently up to him.

Ian's face relaxed into a smile as well, and he said something Arkie couldn't hear over everyone else's conversation. She went into the kitchen for a glass of orange juice, returned to the loungeroom and sat on the stool next to the piano.

"And whose idea was that?" said a voice beside her. Mum wedged herself onto the stool as well and pointed over at Mr Clifton and Ian.

"Mine, I guess," Arkie said quietly.

"Good thinking," mum answered in a contemplative voice, and spent a few moments gazing about roomful of people with quiet satisfaction. "I was talking to Kylie's mum the other day," she said then, "down at the bank. She apologised to me about your last visit to their place. It wasn't very pleasant, apparently."

I don't want to talk about it. "That was ages ago, mum. Kylie's father turned up on the wrong weekend and started arguing with her mum about it. That's all."

"It must have been a bit upsetting for Kylie."

"I guess so."

"Has she talked much about it since?"

"No." *Not to me.*

Mum sighed.

"Why did our dad leave?" Arkie asked.

Her mum looked sideways at her and said, "Because he and I were different people."

"Different how?"

"Because we met at college and married too young. Because we got a bit older and realised

215

we'd each changed. He wanted me to be at home, and I wanted to work. I'd trained for four years to be a teacher, and I'd trained as a musician for most of my life. I couldn't give that away..."

"Do you miss him?"

"Not now," mum said quietly. "Do you?"

Arkie shrugged. "I hardly know him. And Jo doesn't know him at all really. All we know are you and Michael."

"A meal at a restaurant with your dad, once a year, isn't very much, I suppose. I'm sorry for that —"

"Why doesn't he see us more often?"

"Perth is a long way from here, and..." Her mum fell silent, before adding assertively, "Write to him, Arkie. Tell him what you feel."

"What'll he say?"

Mum looked down at her glass of wine. "I don't know. And you won't know yourself until you tell him. Did you want to go and visit him? Stay with him?"

"No. Just see him sometime and, you know... talk."

Mum nodded. "Write him a letter, Arkie."

And he'll be over here next Christmas or Easter as usual, take me and Jo to a restaurant for lunch and say to us, I hope you're doing well at school and I hope you're being a help to your mother.

There was a commotion of scraping footsteps at the doorway, and another group of people arrived. They were carrying large and cumbersome black cases.

"Alan!" mum exclaimed, standing up. "What's

216

happening?" She laughed in mild disbelief, and everyone in the room broke into applause.

"The band's here!" someone called.

"Okay if we set up here?" Alan enquired. Arkie had recognised him as a familiar guest, another of the teachers from high school. She stood up and moved across the room, watching with some amazement as the contents of the cases revealed musical instruments and amplifiers. Skeleton-like, a drum kit was assembled on the floor beside mum's piano, and electrical leads coiled themselves to power points.

"We've just finished a set up at the local in Mona Vale. . ." Alan explained, hitching a guitar strap over one shoulder. He looked as though he'd been perspiring. "Thought we'd call in here for a quick show."

A woman beside him was also strapping on a guitar. She pointed at Arkie's mum and announced, "Susan's joining us on keyboards as from tonight." Everyone began clapping and cheering, as the band members adjusted equipment and tuned instruments. At last, musical notes jumped from the amplifiers.

"As long as I don't have to sing —" mum called above a rising crescendo of drums and guitars.

Michael was sitting at one end of the couch beside a couple of mum's music students, and Arkie wandered over and sat on the armrest next to him. They glanced at one another, exchanging crooked smiles. Mum was at her piano, listening to the first bars of a steady blues song and nodding her head slightly to the beat. Her fingers settled on the piano keys then, and lazy jazz notes tinkled and rang. A few people started dancing and the floorboards vibrated beneath Arkie's feet. She could see Ian and Mr Clifton nearby, and heard Mr Clifton's voice at one point saying, "...you'll have to do some travelling sometime..."

Jo climbed onto Michael's lap as the music changed beat and became more frenzied. "Back in the U.S.S.R...." he chanted softly every few moments, because he recognised the song.

It wouldn't be like this if mum was still with dad and we were in that home unit we used to live in. Dad wouldn't have let it happen.

The music continued loudly for several songs more and then concluded amid applause and congratulations. The band members set their instruments down and drifted into conversations around the loungeroom. A tape on the stereo began playing again, and mum jammed herself into a space on the couch next to Michael. They exchanged murmurs, laughed and kissed.

Arkie's vision blurred and darkened. With annoyance, she found herself falling asleep. Michael eased himself off the couch and carried an already sleeping Jo upstairs.

"You look tired," mum said to her.

Arkie shrugged. "The music was great," she mumbled back. "You were really good, mum."

Her mother smiled warmly and nodded with some satisfaction. "My new part-time profession," she mused. "I played a few wrong notes here and there. We'll never make it onto 'Countdown', but it's going to be great fun, regardless."

And if I write that letter to my dad, can I say so? Dear dad, mum's joined a band. It's something she wanted to do for a long time, you know.

Her eyes began to close again and she felt her body relax. When she blinked awake, Michael was sitting on the couch again, and Ian was asleep, leant up against him. Mr Clifton walked over, his bow tie crooked and his eyes a bit bloodshot. "I have to be away," he told Michael and mum. "I didn't bring the car, so I'm catching buses home. Thanks for asking me along —" He turned to Arkie. "Goodbye. Good luck with high school next year."

Which means I won't see him again. It's always like that with teachers you like.

"I'll send you and Ian a postcard or two when I get to the Northern Territory," Mr Clifton added.

Ian blinked awake and said drowsily, "Mum'll be home soon." He stood up.

"I can walk him home —" Mr Clifton said amongst goodbyes, as a few other people prepared to leave also. The band had begun to pack their instruments back into the black carry cases.

Arkie walked to the top of the driveway, and said awkwardly, "Thanks for teaching us."

Mr Clifton nodded. "It's been great knowing you. Don't let high school turn you into a boring person, Arkie."

"See you on Monday," she said to Ian, and he blinked, nodding a reply.

There was the noise of late-night traffic, neon lights in the near distance and a faint hiss of ocean. Voices in conversation could be heard from the house. Arkie watched as Ian turned and entered the front doorway of the Seaview flats. Mr Clifton walked on down to the main road, turned the corner and disappeared from view.

FOURTEEN

Ian didn't come back to school.

Something added itself up in Arkie's mind, but she didn't quite know what. On the way home from school with Jo, she stopped in at the chemist's and left her roll of film to be sent off for developing. She found Jo up in Checcutti's takeaway, playing a rather listless game of space invaders by himself.

"Hurry up, Jo," she told him, "I want to get home."

"Stiff cheddar," he answered solemnly, not shifting his stare of concentration from the video screen. "I'm nearly — FINISHED!" he said loudly, as the machine made siren and explosion noises. "I might've beaten the top score if it wasn't for you."

Resigned, she shrugged at him. "D' you want to call in at Ian's and see why he wasn't at school today?" she asked.

"Yeah."

They climbed the stairs inside the Seaview units, and knocked at the door to Ian's flat. There was no answer.

"What if his mum's here?" Arkie said.

"What if she is?" Jo replied. "She's okay, I've met her."

221

"When?"

"When I've been down here sometimes on Saturdays and Sundays."

"What's she like?"

"Don't you know her or something?"

"I've never met her," Arkie almost whispered in reply, and they began descending the stairs once more.

Jo shrugged. "She lets us have chips and coke whenever we want and sometimes she gives us money and we go to the shops. And she never says much, just sits watching TV and smoking."

"Wonder where Ian is, then."

"He said he'd come up and play this arvo," Jo said emphatically.

They climbed the steep part of Ramsay Street and let themselves into the house. Jo turned the TV on, kicked his shoes and socks off, and sprawled on the couch. Arkie raided the biscuit tin in the kitchen and went to her room.

When Mum and Michael arrived home, they came inside unusually quiet.

"How was school?" Arkie heard mum asking Jo.

"Boring," he answered. "Miss Sereni kept yelling at us. Ian wasn't at school, and we went to his place this afternoon. He wasn't there, either."

Arkie was at her desk, scribbling answers to homework. The conversation began to distract her when Michael said, "Ian won't be at home for a while, Jo."

"How come?"

"His mum's been unable to look after him, so he's being looked after by someone else."

"When's he coming back?" Jo asked , his voice hurried.

"Soon," Michael answered. "We hope."

Mum came and leant in Arkie's doorway. "How's the homework?" she asked, and walked over to the desk.

"I'm only doing it now to get it out of the way," Arkie mumbled.

"That's a good idea —"

"What's happened to Ian?" She asked the question without looking up.

Mum took a breath. "He's in an emergency care centre. Welfare people called at his place last night when he was there but his mum wasn't. They waited a few hours for her to return, and when she didn't, they took him to be. . . looked after. Glenda, the counsellor from school knew all about it; she told us at lunchtime today."

"Is he coming back?"

"I don't know, Arkie."

"What about his mum?"

"We have to wait and see."

Why couldn't he have come here and stayed the night then, like he has before? His mum'd be back by now. Or maybe she went away again.

Alone once more, she worked through the remainder of the homework and wrinkled her nose with dissatisfaction when she'd finished.

Michael knocked on her door. "Mind if I come in?"

"Sure."

He had a cardboard grocery box in one hand. "I've come to clean out the last of my things. Thought you might like to finally use the desk drawers for your own stuff."

"Oh...yeah."

He knelt on the floor and methodically emptied each drawer's contents into the box — stationery, batteries, brochures, manila folders, photo envelopes were all stacked within. "Sorry it took so long for me to do this," he said.

"S' okay." She paused and looked at him for a moment. "I looked at all those photos and things."

"I know," he replied.

Ian's chair and desk sat empty for several days, before one of the kids asked, "Hey, what's happened to Koh? He's wagging again."

In a matter-of-fact voice, Miss Tregear said, "He'll be away for a few days —"

Then Adam Black called out, "Miss, on Sunday night some people came and took him."

There was a sudden cacophony of voices. "What happened, miss?"

"Yeah, where is he?"

"He is being looked after for a while," Miss Tregear answered, sounding as though she was unwilling to say more.

"He had a bag with him," Adam Black said in a hushed voice, but Miss Tregear had diverted most of the class's attention onto a research exercise from the morning's current affairs programme on television. Arkie forced herself to concentrate

224

on the chalkboard's coloured diagram and Miss Tregear's crisp, neat handwriting, but her gaze wandered again. Above the chalkboard was the last of the wall displays left over from Mr Clifton's time with the class. The graffiti art mural he'd helped everyone put together was starting to fall off the wall.

All my photos. Today has to be the day.

"Wait right here," she told Jo that afternoon on the way home, and walked into the chemist's. She half-expected Jo to wander on down to the space invader machines, but dutifully he sat himself on the shop steps, beside a bargain basket of cosmetics.

She walked directly to the film and photo counter. "Gerhardt," she told the sales assistant, and then tapped her wallet full of money impatiently as he went through the drawer of photo return envelopes.

"Here we are," he said, handing her an envelope that was promisingly heavy. Hurriedly she opened it, looking to see if the photos were actually hers. A glimpse of one of her self-portraits was enough, and she handed the assistant the money and hurried back out into the street.

"What's the big hurry?" Jo asked more than once. "What did y' get at the chemist's?"

"Photos," Arkie replied, as they passed the Parade Hotel and turned the corner into Ramsay Street. "All the ones I took on that old camera."

"Can I see them?"

"Sorry. Not suitable for anyone under the age of ten."

"Are some of them rude?"

Arkie groaned and pulled a face. "You're a grot, Jo. No, they aren't." She hitched the straps of her schoolbag up onto one shoulder and reached into the zip-up pocket of her tunic.

"I'm gonna tell mum you're still wearing earrings to school that she told you not to."

Arkie was busy swapping her Roman coin earrings for her ordinary studs. "Oooh, I'm really scared, Jo."

"Well I will. She told you that if —"

"Jo, I can probably tell mum about how come the box of chocolates Michael bought her is nearly empty, when she's only had a couple herself.

"Aw, what d' you know about it?"

"I've seen you in the kitchen, trying to reach them off the top of the fridge. When she's at yoga on Wednesday nights and Michael's in the lounge-room marking schoolwork. And what about the wrappers I saw crumpled up under you bed when I did the vacuuming on the weekend? So don't try dobbing on me, boy, 'cause I can dob right back on you."

Jo scowled.

"What are you getting so grumpy about, anyway?" she asked then.

"Nothing," Jo answered, letting his schoolbag drag along the footpath and scowling even more.

"I'll show you some of the photos when we get home."

Jo pursed his lips and nodded.

In the quiet of the house, they went into Arkie's room and sat on her bed.

"Come on, come on. Let's see," Jo grumbled.

"Okay, okay," she grumbled back. *Wow, I'm patient sometimes.* She opened the photo envelope and said, "I get first look."

With a breath of anticipation, she pulled out the twenty-four black and white photos. They were glossy and vaguely sticky, and she controlled the impulse to flick through them quickly. Carefully she examined each picture, then passed it on to Jo.

The ones I took of myself, black dress and black tights. My eyes are staring and I look like a scarecrow.

"Hey Arkie, here's the one of me, mum and Michael in bed that morning."

Mum at her piano, concentrating and day-dreaming at the same time.

"Me and Ian playing nan's tennis racquets like guitars! We oughta join mum's band."

Jo acting like a loony. Ian standing like a soldier, with his face looking sad.

"What are those ones of Mr Clifton?"

"That was his last day at school," Arkie said. "Half the class brought cameras in, and Mr Clifton was posing off."

"Wish I'd had him as a teacher. Show us the next picture."

"Hang on, hang on —"

"Carol's and John's house; I hope we go back there sometime."

"We are. Mum said."

The next photo was grey and shadowed, the crevice littered with a motorcyclist's possessions. Arkie looked closely at it for several minutes, picking out the helmet, gloves, polaroid snapshot, and every other object she had found on that rock shelf. *It was spooky, really.*

Jo craned his head across to see. "What's that?"

"A collection of stuff," she said, trying to sound dismissive.

He took it from her and peered closely. "Motorbike stuff," he remarked. "When Michael and me went on John's trailbike, I had to wear a helmet like that." He craned his head over again to look at the photo Arkie had now come to. "Hey, there's Morgan and Ben —"

"Anton, Rowan and Christy," she finished. The five Arcana brothers stood beside their bus home and gazed with dark, distant eyes. *It felt a bit like we were the first visitors they'd had for a long, long time.*

"It'd be great living in a bus like that," Jo said. "Those kids are lucky."

There were other photos, too. Michael marking schoolwork at the kitchen table, mum washing the Batmobile, Jo standing on his head, the home units next door taking shape, and a couple of blurry pictures that hadn't turned out properly. *Like I was standing in a fog when I took them. But all the rest are as clear as daylight.*

When Jo had wandered off to find something to eat, Arkie put the photo of the rock crevice into one of the drawers of her desk. Then she got *Tony Arcana, age ten months* from the Atrocity Cabinet and, walking over to the wardrobe, hauled down

228

her holiday suitcase, unzipped one pocket and slipped the photo inside.

"These are great," Michael told her after he'd slowly thumbed through the photographs. "Especially the portraits." He leaned back in the armchair, and looked through the collection again. On the television screen before him, reporters and film crews had the prime minister bailed up on the steps of Parliament House. The newsreader's voice intoned solemnly. "Some of these," Michael continued, "would look good enlarged and mounted. You've got a great feel for photographing people, Arkie. I'm very impressed."

"The ones of me aren't very good —"

"Stop being so modest," Michael said with a slight smile. "Did you know there's a photography group at the high school?"

"A lady at mum's party told me."

"That lady was Eve Howlett, one of the art teachers. She runs the photography group —"

"I know, she told me. She said I could join next year."

"And?"

Arkie shrugged. "I might."

Mum walked in from the kitchen and collapsed onto the lounge. "Are you guys hungry?" she asked.

"Starving."

"Good." A faint smell of garlic and fresh herbs drifted into the room. "Dinner's on soon," she said, staring at the TV screen and adding, "Lord,

229

politicians are depressing sometimes."

Arkie gathered her photos up, just as Jo bounded downstairs from a shower, his hair wet and his body reeking of talcum powder. "There's a really funny photo of me and Ian at nan's on the tennis court," he announced. "We have to show Ian when he comes back."

"Jo," Michael said quietly.

"Yeah?"

"Ian might not be coming back."

Jo's mouth opened to say something, but no words came.

"We're not sure," mum added, glancing at Michael, "but you may not see him for a while, Jo. You might not see him at all."

"But why?" Jo asked at last.

Mum took a breath. "Like we said before, his mum hasn't been able to take care of him properly. She's been leaving him at home a lot by himself."

"But he can look after himself," Jo said slowly, "and he comes up here and we look after him."

"He's still been by himself a lot, though. Too much. And he's been trying to care for his mum as well, because she needs looking after too. So," she said, grasping Jo's hands and drawing him close so that he was almost sitting on her lap, "what's happened is maybe best for Ian and his mum. Ian's with people who can look after him all the time. And his mum, hopefully, is seeing people who can look after her."

"Will I see him again?" Jo asked.

Mum shook her head. "We don't know, mate."

Jo pulled away from her grip. "He's my

230

friend," he said, shoulders dropping. He turned around, sat down heavily on the carpet and stared blankly at the television screen.

Michael and mum exchanged serious looks. Gathering her photos Arkie returned to her room, sat down on the bed and stared into space for a while.

Jo took himself off to bed unusually early. His bedroom light was still on when Arkie went upstairs later for a shower; Jo was huddled under blankets fast asleep. The pillow was all wet and his eyes looked puffy; a private bout of sorrow no-one downstairs had heard.

"Is he still awake?" mum said to her from the foot of the stairs.

Arkie shook her head.

Mum walked up and into the room. She looked down at Jo for a moment, then leant down and kissed him lightly. He stirred faintly but did not wake.

"He's not very happy," mum said quietly out in the hallway. "Take it easy with him for a little while, Arkie."

Arkie nodded, switching on the bathroom light. *You didn't have to tell me that. I know what it's like.*

She showered until the room was completely filled by steam and the hot water ran out. When she came downstairs, mum and Michael were sitting close together on the couch. A woman's voice echoed softly through the stereo speakers and on the floor at Michael's feet was the box of contents from the desk drawers. He was slowly passing photos to mum.

"You should put all these into an album," mum was saying. "I said that to you ages ago."

He nodded. "I know, I know. I never seem to get around to it."

"Well, I know what to get you for Christmas, then," she replied. There was a growing pile of photographs on her lap.

"You smell of almond skin cream," mum remarked when Arkie sat down next to her. "*My* almond skin cream. I should make you buy your own."

Arkie held two fingers up and rubbed them. "I need more pocket money to do that," she answered hopefully.

Mum rolled her eyes. The photos on her lap were ones familiar to Arkie. *Michael on his birthday bike. In the garden with dad.* Then, *Graduation Ball, the first time I ever wore a bow tie.* And *Ian Koh, Ramsay Street waif —*

Michael had become very quiet.

Mum told him, "We did all we could, Mike," and he nodded a reply.

The stereo's voice echoed on and dimly, Arkie could see the reflection in the TV screen — herself, Michael looking down, and mum turned to him.

Michael passed more photos along. "Sometimes, I saw myself at his age," he said slowly. "I spent a whole year by myself at school once —" He looked at mum and then Arkie. "I sat at the edge of the playground and watched other kids playing. And waited and waited for someone."

Arkie looked at the photos of Michael as a child, and then Ian, until their faces seemed to blur into one person.

FIFTEEN

"We have two lines over here," Miss Tregear was calling across the playground of ranked children. "This class doesn't have a boys' line and a girls' line..."

A few kids were giggling. *Sometimes she sounds just like Mr Clifton used to at assemblies.*

Mrs King stood at the front of the assembled school and looked highly irritated. "Those lines up the back are a disgrace, sixth class. You'll be at high school in a matter of weeks —"

Someone, somewhere was cheering. "Yippee," came a muffled voice from the back row.

"— but in the meantime," Mrs King added, "you're still part of this school. Sean Taylor, if you think that's amusing, maybe you'll find some lunchtime detentions just as funny."

Four more weeks of school assemblies to go. The restless, unruly sixth graders strode off to their rooms. *And then six more years of the same thing in high school. Yuk.*

Arkie's own classroom very gradually lost its clutter and intimacy. From afternoon to afternoon, kids walked around on desk tops removing artwork and projects from the ceilings and walls. Desks were cleaned out and cupboards sorted through. Miss Tregear turned some of her energies to clearing the storeroom of the incredible amount of waste paper and rubbish it seemed to contain.

"Will you be teaching here next year, miss?" someone asked.

"Looks like it," she replied.

"Gee, hard luck, miss."

"You might get to teach my little brother."

"Or my little sister. She's a terror, miss. She smokes more cigarettes than my mum even."

The last of the artwork came down and with it, a painting with *Ian Koh* written on the back. "I'll take that," Arkie said when Miss Tregear read the name out. It was odd hearing Ian's name spoken for the first time in so long, and for an instant the whole class quietened. Arkie folded the painting carefully and stowed it in her bag.

Days and weeks seemed to stretch out infinitely. Miss Tregear tried to relieve the tedium with interesting projects, but a restlessness underlined everything the kids said or did.

"My mum's sending me to that private school," Kylie told Arkie one day.

"That means," Arkie replied, "you have to wear all that uniform. Hat, gloves, stockings."

"Yeah," Kylie said, and there was a tinge of regret in her voice. "Still, I guess I'll get used to it. Besides, Rebecca's going to the same school too, so we'll be catching the bus down each morning. I'll have someone to talk to —"

First time in ages you've talked to me about anything, Kylie Bethel.

"You're going to the high school your mum's at," Kylie remarked.

"Yeah. Me and everyone else."

"Hey, you might even wind up in your mum's class. Or your stepfather's."

"That'd be weird," Arkie said with a slight laugh.

Stepfather? His name's Michael.

At home, she asked him, "Do you or mum know which year seven kids you're teaching next year?"

Michael laughed. "Is our school that organised? Of course not." He pulled a face. "I might even wind up with you in my class."

"Urk," she replied, and poked her tongue out at him.

Stepfather. After all this time, it didn't sound like Michael. Michael was Michael, gradually brightening up once more, cracking jokes and playing records loudly. He was also obsessed with a new scheme. "I'm going to restore the utility," he said one afternoon with school over and a can of beer to help him muse. "It'll look great tidied up — no rust, new paint..." He started washing and cleaning the old car up, and the puddles of dirt and soggy cobwebbing streamed across the cement and down into the garden.

The sounds of his activities reached Arkie in her room, and mingled with the rise and fall of music from mum's synthesiser. *Like church music or something. Maybe mum should be in an orchestra instead of a band.* An electronic percussion beat joined the music. *It'd be good if we could see the band playing somewhere.*

"I guess we could," Michael replied when she asked. "Alan says the band sometimes plays in the afternoons, out in the garden of a pub up at Palm Beach. Kids are allowed, so we might go up and stickybeak at your mum in action."

Mum in action. Like she was at the party, laughing and having a good time. Playing that great music without even trying. The other images that Arkie had in mind were not the sanitised bands in video clips on TV, but the bands she occasionally saw through the windows of the Parade Hotel on Friday and Saturday nights. After a meal out at a restaurant, she, mum, Michael and Jo had sometimes paused outside the rattling windows of the crowded main bar at the Parade to watch the bands thrash out noisy music.

"Looks like hard work," Jo had said, and mum nodded a heartfelt reply.

Mum's given up Monday nights at home and Wednesday nights at yoga classes for band rehearsals. Friday nights, the band's off playing somewhere, so we don't see her so much during the week. She seems really happy.

The music in the loungeroom continued. Jo was outside in the back yard, kicking a soccer ball around with two kids from his class at school. Every so often their voices heightened in brief dispute before subsiding again into indistinct mutters.

"Have you given up computer games?" she asked him one afternoon when she realised that he wasn't stopping off at the machines in the take-away any more.

236

Jo nodded. "I'm saving up."

"What're you saving up for?"

"I don't know," he answered, with all the re-signed world weariness his eight-year-old voice could muster. "I'm just saving up, that's all."

He's different somehow. His room doesn't smell of wet beds any more and he doesn't bug me so much. It's almost like when we were little, played games together and had just moved to Ramsay Street.

There were *Avaliable Now* signs pegged into the newly unrolled turf outside the home units next door. People came up to turn the sprinklers on each day so that the native shrubs would thrive between their bush rock and cement confines. The unit interiors could be sighted through the windows, white and spartan as the inside of a shoebox.

Arkie walked Headley down to the beach at the end of the last school afternoon. Or rather, he walked her, dragging at the end of his leather lead and straining to get closer to the sand and water. Adults and kids were down here in increasing numbers now, a babble of voices and laughter above the cacophony of the waves.

"Hey, Arkie!" Adam Black called, "Where are ya swimmers?" He was standing on wet sand alongside Sean, Eric and a couple of other kids. They all had zinc cream striped across their noses.

"At home," she called back, hiking past with Headley.

"Disappointment!"

"Yeah, don't be a piker, Arkie —"

"It's holidays now. You gotta come down here. We're gonna be here every day from now on —"

She could sight Kylie and Rebecca out in shoulder-high water, shrieking as waves broke around them.

"Come down tomorrow," Adam said.

"Maybe," she replied with a shrug, and walked on.

I need a new costume, anyway. And how do I look in swimmers? Like a rake. She looked quickly down. *Come on boobs, start growing.*

Miss Tregear had said to them, "Drop in and say hullo on your way home from high school."

"Yeah miss, sure miss, see you miss, have a good Christmas," the class had shouted back as they stampeded out of the classroom and the school for the last time.

High school in six weeks. Ages away yet.

Arkie kicked off her black cloth shoes and walked along the warm sand in bare feet, negotiating towels and piles of clothing. "Take it easy, stupid," she mumbled to the dog as he struggled on. She followed the high-tide line, sprinting for a short distance with Headley and then slowing to a walk. *The shells here are always broken. The ones where we camped out down the coast weren't. They were really nice ones, those shells Jo and me collected. They're in the laundry cupboard in a box.* She took in the view of scattered seaweed and plastic, fragmented rubbish in the sand. *Up here, they're broken. Like rubble.*

She climbed the steps at the rear of the beach, emerging in a park that sat across the road from school. Beyond the peak-hour traffic she could sight an empty playground and bare classroom windows. *And next year, I'll be at the bus stop outside the shops with Voula, Adam and all the rest, while Kylie and Rebecca stand at the bus stop over the road, dressed in their funny uniforms and waiting for a bus to take them somewhere else.*

"Come on you," she said to Headley after a pause, and the two of them set off across the park and back towards Ramsay Street.

That's what I have do: buy a new roll of film for my camera.

SIXTEEN

With the windows wound right down, the summer breeze whipped noisily around the car's interior. At the very edge of the suburbs where the toll gates were, the Batmobile queued up along with other cars; vehicles loaded with boats, caravans, surfboards and pushbikes, sweaty motorists and complaining children.

Dear dad,

Through the tollgates and free of the traffic queue, they set off along the expressway. Arkie chewed on the end of her pen and gazed down at the exercise book paper in her lap.

School holidays are here. We're going way out into the country to stay with friends who live in an old farmhouse.

"What are you working on?" mum asked, looking in the rear view mirror.

"A letter."

"Who to?"

"Someone."

Mum nodded, seeming to guess the complete answer for herself.

I've got my own bedroom now. Mum and Michael and I are going to paint it before school goes back. I'm choosing the colour.

Michael waved a cassette in the air. "Anyone for loud music?"

"Yeah, me!" Jo replied enthusiastically from his corner of the back seat.

"Arkie?" Michael asked.

"Fine by me," she answered.

"Go on," mum said with an exaggerated sigh, "only if you and Jo are going to sing along with it, sing in tune."

Michael turned around and whispered to Jo, "Sing in your worst voice."

Jo grinned and nodded.

Mum and Carol have been friends for nearly twenty years. It'd be great having a friend for that long.

A rumble of music filled the car, and Michael's and Jo's voices joined each chorus in slight discord. Mum and Arkie exchanged good humoured looks in the rear view mirror. Mum was tapping her fingers on the steering wheel in time to the music.

When you're in Sydney next, you should come and visit us where we live. Jo and I have told you before what the house is like, but you've never seen it for yourself.

From time to time she glanced up to see paddocks, hills and rivers she remembered from the previous journey. Roadworkers laboured at several points under the sun, working on dismembered stretches of road with shovels and graders. Cars and vans with doors open and bonnets up parked under shade in roadside parks. Semitrailers pulled over onto the dust between the bitumen and the guide posts to let lines of cars overtake.

The photo I sent you is one I took in my own room with a camera Michael gave me. It's a Voigtlander that belonged to his father and it has this time-delay switch on it so you can take photos of yourself.

Insects met their deaths against the increasingly dirty windscreen of the Batmobile, and at municipal pools in country towns, holidaying children clamoured for diving space around the tiled blue water. The cassette desk under the dashboard ejected a cassette with a noisy click and Michael fed back a tape of calmer, quieter music. They drove and drove.

Can you send me back a photo of you? Hope you reply to my letter. Love, Arkie.

The house remained unchanged.

The hills around had yellowed slightly with summer and there were lilac patches of patterson's curse in the paddocks. Everyone gratefully escaped the heat of the Batmobile's interior, to be immersed in the noise of hullos and greetings from Carol, John and Rhys.

"How are you?" mum asked.

"Pregnant!" Carol answered with a broad smile.

"Really?!"

"Twins, I think —"

Arkie watched as her mum and Carol exchanged hugs and laughter. *What would you say if*

242

I asked you about babies again, mum? She and Jo explored the house all over again, reacquainting themselves with its contents and feel. The adults had gathered themselves around the kitchen table, and at one point, Arkie heard John say, "Well, you won't be seeing the Arcanas this time. Jean got married —"

"You're kidding."

"No, word of truth. She got herself married to a guy she met at the local markets a year or so back. She sold the bus and the land, and took herself and the five kids down to somewhere near Coffs Harbour. From what we've heard, it's all working out really well for them —"

When the luggage had been carted from the car to the spare room, Arkie checked inside her suitcase. The *Tony Arcana, age ten months* photo was there, and she had bought a perspex frame for it so that it no longer curled over. *If the Arcanas have gone, then all the stuff in the cave has probably gone, too.*

Trying not to let misgivings dominate her thoughts, she played games in the early evening with Jo and Rhys. Coherent words and incoherent phrases came from Rhys, a skill he had developed in the months since Arkie and Jo had last visited.

"Reminds me of when you learnt to walk," mum said over dinner that night.

"When was that?" Arkie asked.

"We were at the zoo one day," mum replied. "We were sitting on the grass eating lunch —"

"You and dad and me?"

"No, just you and I. And anyway, one minute you were sitting there with vegemite sandwich on your face and the next, you were waddling in circles around me. Well, falling over mainly, but also walking. Nearly."

"What about when I first started talking?"

Mum narrowed her eyes thoughtfully. "Jo's first word was 'car'. I can't remember what your first word was...one week, you were making baby noises, the next — suddenly — you were speaking sentences. It was as though you'd been waiting for the right moment."

"What about me?" Jo asked. "When I started talking?"

"You?" mum remarked dryly. "Once you started talking, you didn't stop. Drove me around the twist, sometimes."

"Aw, I did not!"

"Sorry, Jo," mum said then, running a hand over his bristly head, "only kidding."

"And how does it feel almost being a high school person?" John asked Arkie.

"Weird," she replied.

"Mm, it's like that."

"What would you like to do eventually?" Carol inquired, and then added apologetically, "sorry, I guess you get asked that a lot."

Arkie shrugged. "I don't know yet, I'm thinking about it." *Nan asks me all the time and I keep making up answers: Vet, nurse, doctor, clothes designer. I haven't the foggiest.*

The following afternoon, when Michael, mum,

Carol and John were out on the verandah couch soaking up the sunlight and talking, Arkie set off. She could hear Jo and Rhys playing somewhere, with Jo chanting, "Boo! Boo, Rhys!" and Rhys giggling uncontrollably.

"Keep that hat on," mum reminded her as she passed by the verandah.

"Alright, alright," she replied wearily.

"And be back before dark."

Arkie, reeking of sunscreen lotion, turned and walked away. "Stop nagging me," she said loudly.

"I'm impersonating a good mother," her mum called out.

Grasshoppers buzzed and jumped in the grass. Arkie strode across the home paddock, straddled the fence and crossed the road. Near the trees, the creek had flooded some time in her absence, and cut itself a slightly new course. It took a little walking to find a narrow enough section to cross before she set up the first of the hills. The network of rabbit tracks led her along the route she'd walked several months before, when the ground had been dotted with yellow fireweed. Now the summer grass had taken hold and someone's cows stood a distance away, dipping their heads and chewing lazily. When they saw her, they froze and stared. Arkie stopped also.

The photo in its perspex frame was tucked inside her T-shirt. She looked at the house behind her, already a long way off, at the toy-sized cars beside it and the faint colour of people sitting on one verandah. The sun shone brilliantly, leaving

245

her hair glued in perspiring strands to her forehead. She walked on. Whenever she did pause, she felt that familiar, perfect stillness.

She climbed the second hill, and the outcrop of rock came into sight.

"Now where...?" she said aloud, getting her bearings and eyeing the greys and browns of granite and masked quartz. At last, she picked a path down the slope and the crevices came into closer view. Hills, trees and rambling rusty fences stretched towards the horizon, and she paused to look about. *Is anyone out here?*

Finding footholds in the boulders and stone, she climbed towards the beckoning gap in the rocks. With an expectant breath, she drew level with the crevice, hesitated briefly, and then crouched down and went in.

There was nothing inside. The dusty floor was a mesh of clambering footprints, some the same size as her own, others smaller. Handprints lay in lines and blobs on the dusty rock shelves. No watch, no glasses, no crash helmet, boots and gloves. No colour photo. It had all gone.

Disappointment engulfed her. After hearing John's conversation back in the house she had expected this, but the emptiness touched her nonetheless.

Where is it all now? Where have they found to hide it?

She looked blankly around, feeling the disappointment being overtaken by unease. Like a haunting, she could picture the man's possessions ranged before her on the shelves and she could almost hear the quiet voices of several Arcana brothers as they came to this place to look at, and touch, all that had been hidden here.

She slipped the photo out from under her T-shirt, and contemplated the baby, then the handwriting on the back. Purposefully, she stood the framed picture in the middle of the rock shelf, so that *Tony Arcana age ten months* smiled out into the shadowed light. Then she left.

The paddock below the rocks was flat and easy to sprint over. She didn't make her way back up the slope towards the farmhouse, but kept to the stretch of paddock, since intuition told her that somewhere straight ahead was where the bus had been. *And when the Arcanas ran across this paddock, I could hear their cowbells ringing.* She climbed a slight rise and the driveway she had been down months before came into view. She slowed to a walk, chest heaving and eyes stung with wind. She pulled the wide-brimmed cotton hat off and fanned the flies away from her damp face, before walking on down the driveway. A climb over one locked gate and several fences brought her to where Jean and her five children had lived.

The yard remained, but little within. The bus had gone, leaving a large yellowish patch of grass. The clothesline still swung between its posts, with no pegs to mark their positions along the cord. The open shed was there, but no pushbikes and dinkies were piled inside. Arkie slowly walked around the yard's perimeter.

Pieces of colour caught her eye and she stooped to retrieve two matchbox cars from the dusty ground. These she pocketed thoughtfully; Jo would probably like them. Oddly positioned and probably also forgotten, a plastic laundry bucket sat upended next to the yard gate. She sat down.

So where are you now, Morgan, Ben, Anton, Rowan and Christy? Living in an ordinary house? D'you wish you were back here?

It was eerie, this empty patch of ground, but then it had seemed eerie when Arkie had visited before and met Jean Arcana and her five enigmatic children.

Like something you'd see in a movie or read in a book. And did their mum know they had those things hidden away? Did she have things hidden away too?

The sun's intensity began to subside.

Maybe I can find out your new address and send a copy of that photo I took of you all.

A long time she sat there, thinking and watching. She wasn't sure just how long it had been, except that abruptly, the sun was resting itself close to the hilltops.

And when it's my first day at high school Morgan Arcana, it'll be your first day, too.

She retraced her steps along the dusty driveway, across the paddocks and over the hills then, until the farmhouse came into view, its colours and detail diminishing with the dimming light. From a long distance away, she could see her mother alone on the front verandah. Arkie climbed through the last of the fences and traipsed across the home paddock until the house took up her entire line of vision. Mum was nestled into a corner of the couch, her head resting on one hand. "Hello," she said quietly.

"Where is everyone?" Arkie asked, hoisting herself over the verandah railing and collapsing onto the couch also.

"John, Michael and Jo took themselves off for a walk up to the hill at the back. Carol and Rhys are inside asleep, and I've been here. I could see you from quite a distance away."

"I could see you, too," Arkie replied, unlacing her sneakers and kicking them off, before squirming into a more comfortable position against the cushions.

"Where did you get to?" mum asked.

"Over the top of that hill and around the paddocks."

"See any snakes?"

"No."

"John and Carol warned you to keep an eye out."

"Yeah —" She pulled the hat off and flicked her damp hair away from her forehead. "It's nice around here. I'm glad we came back."

Mum nodded. "Me too."

"How come you and Carol have stayed friends all this time?"

Her mother paused, thinking, and then replied slowly and quietly, "We're really similar people, I guess. Every time we meet, it's like we've never been apart. We're...kindred spirits." She looked at Arkie, and added, "Are you still friends with Kylie?"

Arkie shifted uncomfortably and shook her hand. "No. Not really."

"What happened?"

Arkie shrugged. "She's different. She says

dumb things and other kids take notice of her."
*And kids gang up on each other. Like me, some-
times, and Ian, lots.* She paused. "Anyway, Kylie's
going to a different high school than me next
year."

"What sort of school?"

"A Catholic girls' college —"

Mum said quietly, "Will you miss her?"

Arkie gazed down at the worn verandah
boards. "No," she answered.

Mum sighed and reached a hand out. Arkie
succumbed to the contact, and leant back against
her mother's hugging, enveloping arm. *Why am I
doing this? I feel like a little kid.* "What was it like
when you started high school?" she managed to
ask.

"Awful," mum replied flatly. "I was sent to
boarding school, away from all the friends I'd
made right through primary school —"

"But why?"

"Family tradition. Because nan wanted me to
turn into a particular kind of person, maybe. I
hated being there at first, and spent a whole term
not wanting to have anything to do with anybody.
And then by accident one day, I sat at a desk next
to a tall skinny girl with glasses. Her name was
Carol, and she'd been sent to school away from all
her friends, too. And —"

"Were you goody-goodies, or did you muck up
for teachers?"

"We mucked up, as you've no doubt heard."

"Did you ever think of sending me to boarding
school?"

Mum smiled. "Never. But do you think you'll be able to stand being at the same school as Michael and I?"

"I guess I can."

"I can almost promise," mum said, "that you'll meet up with other kids who are into photography, into finding out about people and places, and who can talk about more than whatever it was they saw on video the night before. Give it time, Arkie." For a moment, their eyes and smiles met. "You remind me of myself, sometimes," mum concluded.

Arkie scanned the view before her — the empty road, the square of paddock where once there'd been a tennis court, and beyond, where there had been an entire town. Somewhere away, birds called in the trees, and the brief stillness that followed enveloped everything like a dream.

In the near distance came a voice, and then another in echoed answer.

"Here come the bushwalkers," mum murmured.

John, Michael and Jo clumped onto the back verandah, bringing a racket of conversation with them, and the house seemed to waken from its dusk dream. Doors were opened, Carol and Rhys emerged from their sleep, and everybody seemed then to be doing circuits around the kitchen in pursuit of glasses of water, cups of tea and food for dinner. Jo insisted on having the television switched on, and the raucous din and falsely animated voices of a TV quiz show filled the lounge-room like an entity that didn't belong to the house.

251

Arkie stayed out on the verandah and took in the sunset, until the mosquitoes drove her inside.

When she did go in, the noise had abated somewhat. The TV's voice was more sober; the evening news was on, and Jo had moved back into the kitchen where he sat on the floor playing a game with Rhys. The four adults were ranged around the table, preparing food, sipping wine from old Vegemite glasses and talking.

She sat down in one of the armchairs and took in the room's darkly panelled walls, the shelves of books, the old stereo in one corner, the little eucalypt tree hung with Christmas decorations, and then the reading lamp next to her, poised like a dancer's hand and spilling dim light all around.

The reception for the commercial TV station wasn't too good, and the news broadcast from the city was traced with an undercurrent of static. The picture veered between crystal visibility and coarse snowiness.

"But what does Christmas mean to children in state institutions?" said the newsreader with polished gravity. "What does the festive season mean to them? Susan Cobcroft filed us this report —"

The picture flickered and then changed; a group of adults and children. Mostly children. The camera took in their faces and actions, presents being torn open, a large garish Christmas tree with decorations.

"Christmas means presents," stated a little girl who was more involved with what she was unwrapping than with the camera being aimed at her face, "lots and lots of presents."

"It means food," said the little girl beside her, staring earnestly at the camera, "yummy stuff like sweets and chips and things."

The camera found another face, and Arkie's mouth dropped open in silent surprise.

"I got a new pair of sneakers," said the child on TV, sweeping tassels of hair from his face and speaking in a voice so familiar that Arkie could not find her own, "and a pocket computer game. I always get good presents at Christmas. My mum always bought me stuff —"

"You liar, Ian," Arkie found herself whispering, without malice. "Jo —" she began to say, "Jo. Michael —"

But the noise of conversation and laughter from the kitchen was too loud for her to be heard. Intently, she watched the TV screen, and Ian's face looked back at her, forlorn and distant. The camera lingered a moment longer as he added, "Christmas should be every day."

The newsreader's face reappeared, and Ian — his voice, his face, himself — was gone. It had all happened in an instant, and then the television picture and sound were obliterated by static.

"Useless thing," John said goodnaturedly, as he strode into the room. "It's hopeless trying to watch it sometimes. Were you watching anything?"

"No...no, not really," Arkie replied in a dazed voice. "It was only the news."

John flicked the TV switch and the screen blackened into silence. "D' you mind a bit of music instead? I might put a tape on."

253

Arkie shrugged a reply. "That'd be nice."

John rifled through piles of cassettes, eventually found one, and inserted it into the tape deck. He knelt down, waiting for it to start playing.

When the music did start, it was softly and hesitantly — a piano by itself, and then a tinkling undercurrent of synthesiser that built up decisively into a shimmering bank of music. Without warning, voices filled the music's backdrop, calling-out, answering-back, conversational voices that belonged to two children.

"Hey," Arkie realised, "that's Jo and me. This is one of mum's tapes."

John nodded. "She mailed it to us — oh — a couple of years back. One of my favourite tapes, actually." He stood up. "Dinner's going to be ready soon," he added with a smile, and clumped back into the kitchen.

The sky outside had the last hint of sunset colour about it. *Sometimes it feels like I'm by myself even when I'm surrounded by people.* Arkie looked down at the loungeroom floor with its clutter of toys and newspapers. Music rang out softly from the stereo speakers, and with it, snatches of her own voice and Jo's as well, small squeaky children's voices from another point in time. *What game were we playing and what were we talking about? I can't remember.* She stared back at the TV screen, and heard another voice join the music's backdrop. *Hey Ian, you were there, too. We were probably kicking the soccer ball around, and you were missing half the shots.*

"Arkie." Mum's voice from the kitchen.

"Arkie." Michael's as well.

254

"I'll find her," Jo said then, and he jogged into the loungeroom. "Hey, Arkie —"

She was sitting on one armrest of the couch and Jo ground to a standstill, sensing he had disturbed something. "Dinner's ready," he said more quietly, and gazed at her with expectant eyes.

"Okay," she replied.

Behind her in the kitchen, the conversation heightened into uproarious laughter, inviting and beckoning.

Great, Arkie thought to herself, *this meal is going to last for ages and I might even get to say something. There are things I can talk about and tomorrow, I'm getting my camera out of the suitcase and taking some new photos.*

Slowly and deliberately, she went to join everyone around the table.